ADIRA: MISSION TRITAN

VINAY GUPTA
CHIMAKURTHY

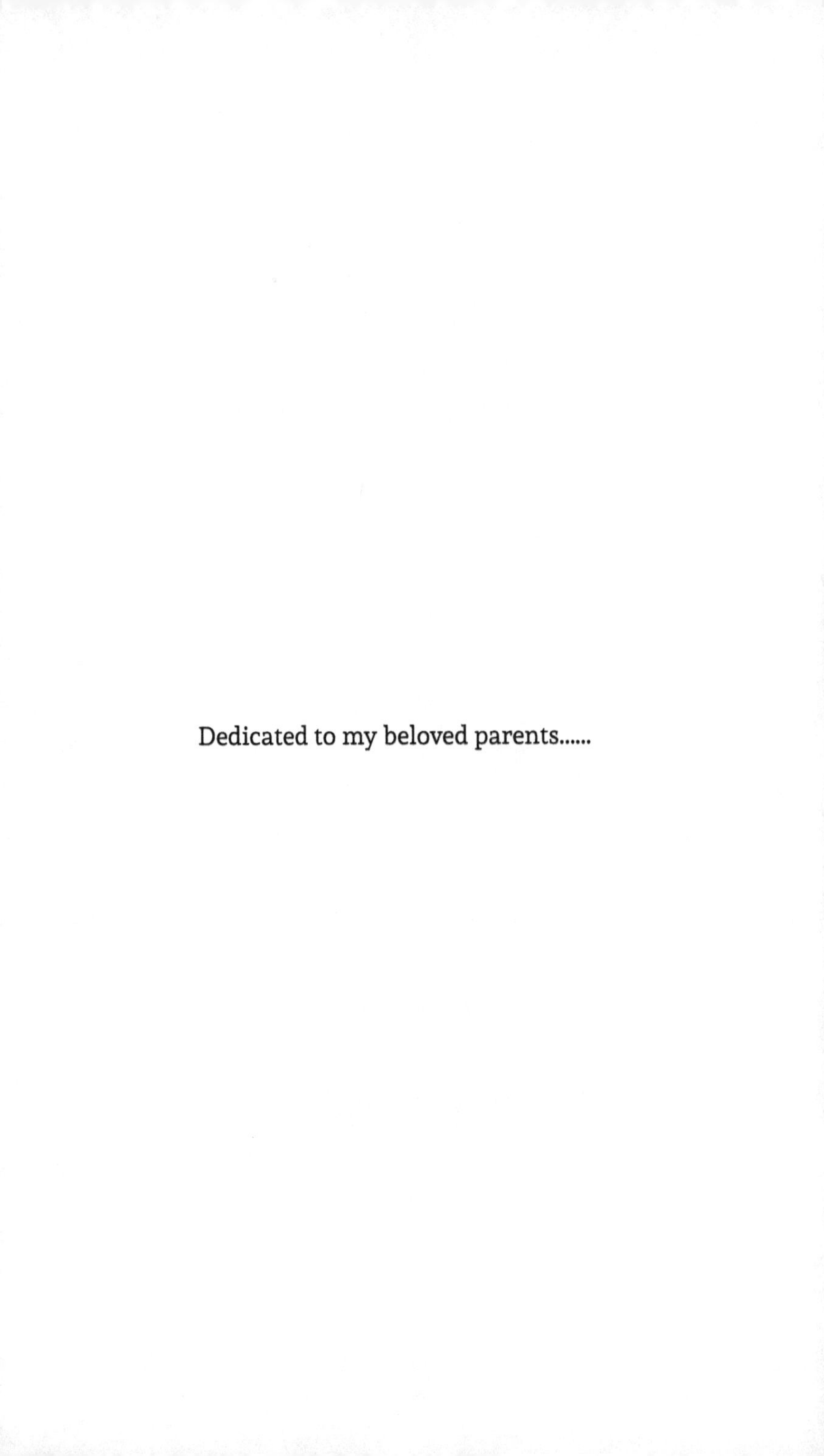

Dedicated to my beloved parents......

Contents

Prologue

After saving the Aqualeans from the evil alligator, I thought everything was set and we could live happily ever after, but very soon an incident developed that needed my utmost attention. After regaining consciousness, Marino's wristband indicated there was something we needed to take care of, and it was serious.

We looked into the issue and found that Marino's father, the king of Tritas and my father's best friend, was missing, and we were unable to track him on the screen. Now my mission was to find him and bring him back to his kingdom. I had to find the cause of his disappearance as soon as possible.

ONE

FOUR MEMBER TEAM

'Good morning, Princess Adira.'

Good morning, beloved guest, Prince Marino.'

Hey Cali,' said our security chief, Milo.

I said, 'A very good morning to you Milo. May I know why you are here?'

He replied, 'I am here to assist you and your next mission. Your father, our king ordered me to be with you and help you until the completion of the mission.'

I said in return, 'Thank you for your concern, but we three are fine. We are not on the mission yet. Just thinking how to start, where to start, and when to start.'

Milo said, 'Princess, it's my duty to protect the royal family. Our king ordered me to protect and help you.'

Marino responded, 'Adira, it is okay. Let him be with us. He is a loyal person. Moreover, he is a well-trained royal security head. I tend towards your father's decision that he will assist us and protect us throughout our journey. I am not in a position to take risks in protecting you. So, please do not say no.'

With that, I was not able to speak a single word against him. I said, 'Okay, Milo, you can join our team but on one condition. You have to follow my orders. Is that okay for you?'

He said, 'Yes, my Princess, I am here to help you and protect you.'

'You are also a team member, so we are like the four directions in this world. Sit down and welcome to the team. We three were discussing our plan in my living room. Now with Milo, our team has become a four-member team.'

'First, I will explain the details of what happened yesterday for the sake of clarity. I will also explain the plan for our mission. Yesterday, we made the gems one single gem with a special procedure documented in the scrolls and books. This was done by our grand advisor. I am not going to explain the gem union; it is a beautiful experience that can't be explained.

Later, after the reunion and placing the gem in its designated position, Marino's wristband gem suddenly appeared and started blinking peculiarly. I asked our grand advisor what had happened and the meaning of that indication. He saw the band clearly and said, either his family or the kingdom is in danger. He also asked the screen to show his kingdom and his father.

Unfortunately, the screen didn't show his father's location, but we could see the kingdom of Tritas, it was on the verge of danger. He also said that someone from outside his kingdom should save it and his family. Later, I asked the screen many times for the solution and the location of his parents.

The icy screen in our secret and sacred chamber showed only his mother's location. The solution shown was to travel from Aqualean to Tritas. We were to travel in a huge carriage with four dots on it, indicating the four members. Yesterday, I could not understand the fourth member, but now I realized that the member was Milo.

This was the only information available to us. Now coming to my plan, we four members would start off in the afternoon in a special carriage pulled by eight high-speed whales. It was equipped with all sorts of food, weapons, safety gear, gems, counter-safety measures, and much more.

I asked the remaining members for suggestions. This time before Cali, Milo reacted and said, 'Princess, it is not safe to go alone to that kingdom as we do not know what has happened. There may be an inter revolt of the citizens, or some royal employee could have betrayed the king or tried to steal the gem protecting the kingdom. There are many ambiguities.

My suggestion was to take our army there and sort the issue out. Fearing assassination, Marino's face became pale and dull. I said nothing will happen to king Tritan. I will protect him and bring him back. This was my promise to Prince Marino. With that, his dullness reduced a little but he didn't speak.

Cali started speaking, however. 'Princess, my suggestions are that we will take at least one hundred soldiers with us just for the safety of the people and the royal family. We will be on a mission to find out what happened and to save Prince Marino's father and their kingdom.'

I said in response, 'Yes, Cali, your suggestion is good. We will be moving on with the mission now. In the evening, gather all the resources to come behind us. Also, instruct the guards to go to the palace directly and give protection to Prince Marino's family.'

'Now everyone, go and pack your things and get ready for the mission. I will meet with the grand advisor for any suggestions.'

Cali and Milo went out on my instruction. Only Marino was left in the room. I turned towards him and said, 'Marino, don't worry about your father. As I said previously, I will find him and bring him back to you as soon as possible. It's my promise to you.' I placed my hand on his hand. He didn't speak a word - just nodded his head as a sign of agreement.

I also said, 'Go take some rest till the afternoon. We will start our journey after lunch. He went to his room. I stood to meet the grand advisor for information regarding the situation. Fortunately, he came to my room and said, 'Good morning, Princess.' I replied, 'Good morning grand advisor, come sit down. I was about to come and ask about the Tritas kingdom - its strengths and weaknesses - and your idea of what had happened there.'

He said, 'Princess, here is my idea. King Tritan has been kidnapped and the gem stolen. An alternative gem of a smaller size was placed there for the protection of the palace and the people. I believe King Tritan is still alive. I think a very high-level official helped do it.'

I asked him, 'High-level official means chief advisor, royal security head, or even members of the extended royal family. I still don't understand why they kidnapped the king.'

The grand advisor replied, 'There are many reasons for kidnapping the king. As in every kingdom, there are direct and indirect agents. All royal secrets are known to very few persons in the kingdom. So, I believe there may be huge assistance from inside Tritas.'

I asked, 'Can you suggest anything to rescue King Tritas and save Tritan.'

He said, 'Yes my Princess, I am here for that purpose. I suggest three points: the first is not to believe anyone, including their chief royal security head, grand advisor, or members of the royal family. Act like you are listening and following their suggestions, but do only what is necessary.

The second thing I want to stress is that the person doing all this knows that someone will come to rescue the king and the kingdom. There may be traps in and around the kingdom or maybe on the path you travel, so be very careful while on the journey.'

'The third thing is related to the second one. there is a book in our library on the known traps in the Ocean. There are many traps and the escape mechanism is explained in that book. The book was written by your ancestors to pass on knowledge to future generations. Go grab the book and follow the methods suggested. They should be very helpful to you on your journey. That's all I can suggest, my dear Princess.'

I said, 'Thank you, grand advisor. You have given me a lot of very helpful input. Definitely I will keep in mind all your suggestions. I will go now to the library to gather the book.'

He said, 'Okay then, princess, I will take my leave for now. I have a meeting with your father regarding this issue. All the very best, Princess Adira.'

I said, 'Thank you, grand advisor.' He left the room, and I deeply thought about the culprit in the kingdom of Tritas. Now I have to grab the book suggested by the grand advisor, and I shall not believe anyone.'

I went outside my room and entered the corridor. Cali joined and asked, 'What happened in the meeting with the grand advisor?

I said, 'My dear, he stressed three points and suggested I grab a book in the library. Now I am going there; where are you going?'

Cali said, 'I came in search of you. I will join you in search of the book.'

I said, 'Come on, Cali, we both shall go there. Time is running out and we have to hurry. Did you arrange the things required for our journey?'

Cali replied, 'Two large carriages full of food, gems, javelins, protective equipment and two small carriages with six whales pulling each carriage. In one carriage, our four team members will be accommodated while the similar carriage will accommodate Prince Marino's personal assistants.'

We reached the library and Cali said, 'Princess, shall we go down to the icy screen and seek help.'

I said, 'Okay, Cali, I always follow your advice. Let me open the door.' We both entered the underground secret chamber. I said, 'Do you have any specific plans for this mission or do you doubt the sources?

She said, 'We know very little and will sort things out. Don't worry, my dear princess.'

We stood near the icy screen and asked about the location of Prince Marino's father. The screen showed a dot but no location specified. We understood that he was still alive but the screen was unable to trace the exact spot. Then I asked the screen how to rescue him. As for the route between Aqualean and Tritas, the screen showed two paths leading to two different locations: one in the south direction and the other to the east.

I have asked the screen for more information, but it showed nothing further. We also asked for a plan or things we might need before the rescue mission. The screen showed four members in the carriage moving towards Tritas. But we saw only three members returning to Aqualean. We understood that Marino would not be returning.

Cali and I tried different questions and ended up with the screen repeating its image. So, we decided to work with our plan, based on the information available. Cali and I started moving; suddenly I said to Cali, 'Go up, look after the arrangements, and pack everything. I will be back in a couple of minutes.'

Cali said, 'As you wish, my dear. Complete your work quickly and go to your room. I will be packing your things there.' She went up and I came back to the screen. I had doubts that the screen would show four persons going there and three persons returning. Was Marino staying back or something dangerous was cooking up in the process of this rescue mission?

I asked the icy screen, 'Is Prince Marino staying back at his palace after the completion of the mission?' The screen showed the palace and the entire kingdom with no sign of Marino. I asked about the persons returning from Tritas to Aqualean after the successful completion of the mission. The screen only showed the three dots in the carriage.

I asked the screen who would be going on the rescue mission. It showed the faces of our four-member team: Marino, Cali, Milo and me. We are a four-member team but from Aqualean, we are eight in total going to Tritas. The screen didn't show them all. I had to look into the issue. I shouldn't reveal this information to anyone until I got clarity on it.

I finally asked the screen, 'Is there any threat to the life of anyone in our four-member team?' Oddly, the screen showed nothing, only a blank screen. That meant the screen was not responding to my question or everyone might be safe on this mission. I needed to find answers to this question.

I went up and the door closed automatically. I looked at the scrolls and books in the library. I finally found the book suggested by the Grand Advisor. My search didn't stop there. I went on searching for more books and scrolls related to my mission. Finally, I got tired and stopped looking.

Cali came inside the library and said, 'My dear princess, why are you still here? Time is running out; we have to look after so many things before we take off.'

I said, 'Finally, I found the book recommended by our Grand Advisor. I am also trying to find new information regarding our mission.'

Cali said, 'Princess, get some rest here and I will search for you.' Cali searched thoroughly but didn't find anything. She sat for some time and she started searching again. Behind the racks was a disguised door. She was curious and said, 'Look, my dear, what I have found.'

I was so excited. We forcefully moved the heavy rack, but the door didn't open. I took my javelin and touched the door. We were both surprised at what happened after that. All the walls of the room turned into a self-illuminated design. The door depicted a pattern that was different from the walls. Previously, this is an old, yet beautiful room. Now it had turned into a self-illuminated room.

I pushed the door with my right hand while holding the javelin in the left one. I entered the room and Cali followed me. I was impressed and mesmerized by the beauty of its architecture. Inside the room, we found a world of books on four floors.

I said to Cali, 'I think my parents and the Grand Advisor never knew about this. We can get the information we want in here but we didn't know what kind of books were on each rack.' Cali looked around for something to help us find the right books.

Soon she came across icy screens in many places. We both approached one screen and asked for books regarding the kingdom of Tritas. The screen displayed many books, but one hooked me to it: The Five Mysteries of Tritas. I touched the image of the book with an icy hammer and it showed the exact place. The screen also showed an option to deliver the book to us. I didn't want it delivered because I wanted to check out the arrangement. I walked through the central corridor of the room and found stairs. I climbed them. I was amazed at the detailing of another floor. The illumination and placement of books were amazing while the delivery mechanism was very far ahead of its time.

This was the power and art of my ancestors. There might not be a definite solution to our problem. I reached the rack specified by the icy screen and located a suggested book. I took it into my hand from the second row at the bottom of the rack. I sat there and looked at the book from the outer cover.

It looked very old. There was a palace on the cover and four circles in the four corners. I was about to open the book when Cali shouted, 'Princess, I have found the book we have been searching for.' I quickly closed the book in my hand and came to Cali, who said, 'Princess, look at the screen. I have found Ocean Traps. There are many books related to the topic and I chose this one.'

I said, 'I always go with you, Cali, so grab it. You have to hit that button with the hammer.' She pressed the button and suddenly a sound could be heard and the book came to the desk near the icy screen. We were overwhelmed by the arrangement and delivery of the books.

I said, 'Cali, we shall come here later after the completion of the mission and spend some time looking into every detail. Let's go with these two books.' She nodded her head. We both left the vast library and the door closed by itself. I thought I relate this piece of information to my parents and the Grand Advisor.

I said to Cali, 'My dear, a small change in our schedule. We shall start in a couple of hours. Go to Prince Marino's room and inform him of the updated time. Also, tell him that we shall go for lunch in half an hour. I will be waiting for him in our dining hall.'

Cali went to Price Marino's room while I went to my parent's living room. Fortunately, both my parents and the Garand Advisor were talking. My mother saw me and started crying. she caught my hand.

She said, 'My dear, I don't like your personal involvement in this mission. Many people can complete it, including Milo. She hugged and kissed me on my forehead and said, "Remember my dear, we have seen your courage in your last mission, you almost left us. It made us cry a lot and by the Ocean God's grace, you came back to us. This time, I don't want to lose you again. Please don't go, my dear.'

I said, 'Don't worry, Mom, nothing will happen to me. I will be back soon, and this time we are going with Milo. Not only Milo but we are also taking four of the personal assistants of Prince Marino. I will be fine and return safely.'

I went near to my father and said, 'Dad, today we discovered a huge library in our palace in the forbidden room.' My father and the Grand Advisor were both excited; their faces started to glow. I said, 'There is a door behind one of the racks and the door opened with a special gem acquired from Mount Kea.'

The Grand Advisor said, 'In my childhood, I heard many stories regarding this library which is one of the biggest in the entire Ocean.' Your father and I searched there many times and never found it.'

I said, 'I am in a hurry now and couldn't explore it much. I just took a couple of books. I was very impressed by the construction. It is far ahead of our present design.

My father said, 'Take all the required things for your journey and the military will follow you tomorrow morning.'

I said, 'We will start in the early evening, Dad. Come, let's have lunch together.' We all moved to the dining hall while I instructed Cali to inform Marino to come to the dining hall to join us. Marino came to the hall and we sat for lunch.

I sat beside Marino. He was not talking about anything, just looking sad. I turned towards him and said, 'Hey, Marino, I can understand your feelings but you cannot change the situation. Only actions will do. We are going to rescue your father as I have promised; moreover, you're not eating properly. Have something as we have a long journey ahead.' Everyone completed their lunch.

I stood and walked towards my parents and said, 'We are set for the mission and will start in a couple of hours. My parents stood and my Father said, 'Look, my dear, if you require anything from Aqualean at any point, please don't hesitate to contact me. For now, be safe.'

I nodded and went to my room with Cali and Marino. I said to Marino that we had found two books to help on our mission in a huge library in the forbidden room. Marino turned towards me and said, 'Next time I too will join you in the library.'

We reached my living room and sat down. I confirmed with Cali that all the requirements were fulfilled. Cali said, 'Princess, as far as I can remember and as per your orders, everything is set. Milo came to my room and wished me well.

He said, 'Princess, the whales, carriages, Prince Marino's personal assistants and all security persons are ready for our departure.

I said, 'Okay Milo we shall start our mission very soon, so please be seated.'

Milo said, 'Princess, if nothing is important to discuss, we shall start our journey.

I replied, 'We are just reciting the requirements and arrangements.' We stood as team members and moved to the central hall to meet my father and take his blessings. My father was on his throne. We bowed before the king. I walked towards him and said, 'Father, we will be starting our journey, so please bless me.' He stood, blessed us and wished our team all the best.

He said, 'I hope to see you all back with my best friend, Tritan. We four members moved out of the hall and proceeded towards the carriages to start the journey.

TWO

MISSION TRITAN

The four members reached the carriages. Marino's assistants were waiting for us and they bowed. Marino asked, 'Is everything packed and set for our journey?' They nodded, and one person said, 'Yes, Prince Marino, we are good to go.'

The four assistants of Prince Marino got into one carriage and we four got into another one. Milo took the reins and looked at me for the signal to start. I blinked as an indication to start. He pulled the reins and our journey started towards the kingdom of Tritas.

I turned towards Marino and said, 'Now you should be glad as we are one step ahead in rescuing your father and setting everything right in Tritas. Don't worry about anything. As soon as we reach Tritas, you can take charge and look after official matters. We three will continue the mission and bring back your father.'

Marino said, 'Nothing doing. I intend to be part of this mission. Official matters will be taken care of by my mother.'

I said, 'Okay, Marino, come with us. I can understand your feelings towards your father.' We traveled for a couple of hours and not much was discussed in the carriage.

Then Milo said, 'Princess, is this the way you traveled in carriages on the previous mission? Everyone is calm and silent.'

Cali replied, 'No, not this way, Milo. We were very enthusiastic and energetic.'

I asked Milo, 'Let me ask you something: what is the plan of action now? How do we rescue King Tritan.'

He replied, 'Princess, first we go to the palace and restore the bubble to the maximum possible extent. After that, we will enquire to secure information regarding this issue."

I asked him, "How do you select the persons for the inquiry?"

He replied, 'It is very simple Princess. First, we randomly select persons from the palace along with some security personnel working there. One more thing: we should keep in mind that we must deal with the royal family members carefully and tactfully."

I said in reply, 'Yes, I understand. It is a very sensitive issue and we should take care.' I turned towards Marino. He nodded his head in agreement. I wanted to bring his mood back to a normal state so I cracked some jokes. He giggled a little. Cali and I looked at each other's faces. She drew near to me and whispered something. I laughed a lot. Marino asked me what had happened.

I didn't reply but secretly took a normal red gem and prayed for the moody man in the cabin. Soon after, an underwater wave hit us. Cali and I had prepared for that. Milo was not holding anything back. He fell from his seat and rolled on the floor of the cabin. Marino started laughing aloud and said, 'Someone catch him and make him stop that rolling.'

Cali and I looked into each other's eyes and blinked. I said, 'Cali, stop him. Make him settle down.' Cali did the job. He composed himself and sat in his place.

He said, 'The jerking was so bad and I could not manage to stay seated, so I fell.' None of us spoke for a moment.

I said, 'Shall we take a break here as we started at least three or four hours ago?

Marino said, 'Yes, we shall take a break.'

I called upon Milo to stop the whales from running. I said to Cali, "Go look to see if it is safe for a break. Tie the carriage if you feel it is safe.' Cali took a gem and attached it to the roof of the carriage. It made the bubble bigger so the whales are in the water.

The four of us got down to look around. Milo said, "We shall stay here for the night as this place is wonderful. The waters are calm, so we will be safe."

I said, "As you wish, Milo, we shall stay here for this night." Milo and Cali arranged the set up quickly, as our carriage was bigger compared to the one we had used on our last mission. It had many more facilities.

Marino and I sat down in the outdoor setup. There were four chairs and a beautiful outdoor table. The table and chairs were white and decorated with pearls. There were rare red and blue gems to top it off. I felt like I was in our palace with my best friends.

I turned towards Marino and said, "Marino, what are the best places in your kingdom and have you ever constructed anything interesting in recent years?" Marino didn't answer. Meanwhile, Cali and Milo came out with some special dishes made just for us.

Cali asked me, "Did we disturb your privacy? Shall we wait inside the carriage?"

I said, "Nothing like that Cali. Please join us. I am only asking Prince Marino about Tritas."

Marino said, "Its nothing like Aqualean, but there are places near Tritas that should interest you. I will take you all there. Unlike Aqualean Palace, the one in Tritas has square towers and no slides around it. Moreover, you have eight towers, and we have only five. Over all, the total kingdom is not as big as Aqualean."

I said, 'That's fine, Prince Marino, each kingdom should have a different construction and outlook so it depicts their culture. After completion of this mission, we will establish an innovation center in Tritas headed by Prince Marino.'

We four talked a lot about many topics like the alligators' return, improving our gadgets and acquiring more powerful gems, etc. We enjoyed a wonderful and delicious dinner, and I thanked Cali and Milo for such mouth-watering food. We arranged our stay that night outside the carriage because it was very near to Aqualean, and we are very confident that we were safe.

The next day morning, we restarted our journey very enthusiastically. I said, 'Look, my dear friends, how wonderful it is that on the last mission, we traveled in the northern direction from Aqualean and for this mission we are traveling in the southern direction. We are traveling exactly opposite now."

Today Cali was riding in our carriage, and I said, 'My dear friends, from today till the completion of this mission, be alert all the time and look after each other. We are traveling in the southern direction for seven hundred miles from Aqualean. Till now we have covered only one hundred miles. I believe we will be there in two to three days depending upon the Oceanic conditions.'

Milo said to me, 'Yes, princess, what you have said is right. We have to be very careful from here on. Today we will be out of Aqualean's reach. One more thing I want to ask is did you plan anything to rescue King Tritan?'

After reaching the kingdom of Tritas, we will enquire individually with everyone in the palace and people randomly selected who are connected with the king both directly and indirectly. Meanwhile, we will send a troop of soldiers to search completely and thoroughly in the palace and the town. I believe our soldiers will start today from Aqualean.

Milo replied, 'Yes, my princess, they will start now and will be coming in batches in five carriages, each comprising twenty soldiers. Each troop has one head. Yesterday I spoke to the heads and said, 'Be alert during the journey, and if any one troop misses the course, do not wait for them. Come to the Tritas Kingdom without wasting time. I need at least one or two troops urgently to help us on this mission."

I said, 'Very good, Milo, you have given the correct instructions to them.' I turned towards Cali and said, 'My dear, you are the person who will always be ready with an optimum solution so what is your suggestion for this rescue mission.'

Cali replied, 'Princess, I strongly believe that King Tritan was kidnapped for a reason - a motive initiated by the alligator.' Soon I asked, 'How come it is an alligator this happened soon after the battle in Aqualean? How can he go there, traveling seven hundred miles in a couple of hours?'

Cali replied, 'Princess, that is what we have to figure out. If it is the alligator or its allies, what is their plan and how did they kidnap the king, and where are they hiding.' Marino asked me. 'Why they have chosen us? Why only Tritan?'

Cali said, 'Prince, do not worry, we will figure out everything soon.'

We took a break that afternoon to have our lunch in the moving carriage but our whales needed to rest for a while and we had to feed them. So, we chose a beautiful place and pulled over for a short break. Cali and Milo fed the whales and looked all over the belts, reins and carriage for any damage. We sat at a table outside the carriage but inside the bubble to complete our lunch. The assistants in the other carriage also halted for lunch.

After some time, one of Marino's assistants came and asked Marino, 'My dear Prince, do you need anything from that carriage or from the Ocean?' He replied, "Nothing is needed. All the required things are here in this carriage. One more important thing is to be very careful from here on and follow us with your full attention. Monitor our carriage with utmost care and do not distract us from the course.'

He nodded and took permission from Marino to leave. I said, 'You have given the right instructions to them Marino.' Okay, friends, we are good to go and I have instructed Cali to move the carriage.

I said to Cali, 'Move slowly from here till we halt tonight. Meanwhile, we shall discuss the plan of action right now.'

Milo said, 'As soon as we reach there, I will take a few guards and search the palace first and then the town for the king. The search may be completed by their guards, but I will try to find a clue to this mystery.'

I said, 'My idea is that after reaching there, Milo will go searching as he said. Prince Marino, will be the acting king and look into official matters that need his attention. Finally, we two are left behind. We will meet Prince Marino's family and start our inquiry from that point.

Later, we will meet their grand advisor and royal security head and anyone of interest.'

Cali replied, 'Perfect Princess, I will go with your idea. If nothing goes beyond our control, we shall stick to this plan. One more thing I want to add here is that after our inquiry in the palace and around the town, we shall go out of the kingdom and search for King Tritan.'

I said, 'Yes, Cali, we three – you, Milo, and I - shall go the places I suspect they must be hiding with the captured king.'

Cali said, 'Oh, Princess, you know the places where to go beyond the Tritas kingdom? You are ahead in planning this time around.'

I said, 'Before starting our journey, I requested the icy screen to reveal probable places for searching him. As the screen couldn't locate the king, I reiterated my query for a possible way to solve this mystery.' I asked Prince Marino, 'Do you know any probable places where we can find these captivators? Or do you suspect anyone in your kingdom or outside it?'

He replied, 'No, Princess, sorry. I do not know anything about that, but I heard about some places around our kingdom that are weird. I have been never there and cannot confirm that they exist.'

I said, 'No worries, Prince Marino, we will unveil this mystery and bring your father safely back to Tritas kingdom. Cali, please look for a safe place for our night break, as we are far away from the borders of Aqualean. I suggest we watch ourselves round the clock. We have four members in the other carriage so make them into two pairs to share the time equally to secure our safety.

Milo responded, 'Yes, Princess, I will instruct them to guard us this night. One more thing is that we have countermeasures ready in these carriages that can be activated.'

Cali said, 'My dear, Prince Marino, all the safety countermeasures were already in active mode right from the beginning.'

Cali pulled the carriage to a safe and beautiful place, and the other carriage stopped behind us. This time Cali made a bigger bubble than the day before, and we all alit for the night break. I got down and looked around, amazed to see the beauty of the ocean. Colorful fish were moving rhythmically in groups and the flora was much more beautiful than I ever imagined. Meanwhile, everyone got down and Marino instructed his assistants to be alert. They were divided into two groups and guarded the premises in rotating shifts till the morning.

As usual, Marino and I sat at a table outside the carriage. Cali and Milo brought us delicious food to enjoy. Cali asked me how the dish was. I said, 'I have never tasted such food in my life.'

Cali reacted, 'This is a special dish made by Milo with special ingredients sourced locally. Tasty fish with a combination of coral leaves stewed with the required ingredients brought from Aqualean.'

I thanked Milo for such a wonderful dish and took a walk with Marino. I gave him some moral support and wanted to tell him the secret I had seen on the icy screen: only three out of four will be returning back after the completion of this mission. But he was already in so much grief, and I didn't want to increase it. I don't know with whom I should share the information. I knew that Marino would be safe as per the icy screen.

Other than Marino, there was a missing person in one of four persons. Who would it be? Cali, Milo, or me! How to rescue that person from the unknown danger. So many questions were revolving in my head. Only time and effort would give me the answer to this; until then, I would not reveal the secret to anyone.

We four members slept outside the carriage and Marino's assistants guarded us that night. I closed my eyes. So many questions came in front of me and I was thinking of solutions one by one. Thinking about the solutions, I went into a deep sleep. As usual, I woke early in the morning and got ready very fast. I asked the icy screen about my never-ending doubts. This time, showed me one extra image that I hadn't seen before. It was a picture of myself with a bright gem in my hand and a huge tree in my background. The gem was not the one with me at present. The icy screen is suggesting to acquire that gem first.

Later when everyone woke, we were ready for our final day journey to Tritas. Cali took the reins into her hands and looked into my eyes. I blinked as a signal to start the journey. She pulled the reins so hard and the whales started very fast. I said to Milo, 'We are near Tritas; by evening we will reach it. Stick to the plan. If anything shows up suddenly, act accordingly and don't wait for my orders or anyone else's .'

We traveled for a couple of hours at a very faster pace with the other carriage following us. I was discussing some techniques with both Milo and Prince Marino. Suddenly a huge sound disturbed us. Our carriage was hit by a huge rock from the front, and we all fell from our positions. Everyone composed themselves and looked around. The front portion had squeezed smaller, but luckily Cali fell backward and looked fine. Soon I approached Cali and gave her my hand to wake her up. I asked her how she was.

She replied, 'I am fine, but I still don't understand how this happened. I couldn't see anything outside from the driving window.'

We four got down and looked around for the cause; soon the second carriage approached and stopped. They got down and moved toward us. They asked the Princess what happened and was everyone fine?' I just nodded and said, 'Stay alert with your weapons.'

I slowly moved towards the front side of the carriage and was surprised to see what had happened. The remaining three team members followed me. Marino said, 'Adira, what is this, nothing is here so how come the carriage is damaged.'

I said, 'We have to look because the whales have gone ahead. Due to the force of the impact, the belts broke. Only the carriage stopped and was damaged badly.'

Cali went near the crashed area and touched it. She waved her hand towards the water there. She shouted, 'Princess, there is a wall preventing us form moving forward. She also said the wall was invisible.

I moved forward and after a few steps, I fell. Soon Cali and Marino came towards me and helped me get up. Milo ordered the security to arrange for a large, strong bubble and instructed them to look around the perimeter with the two small carriages with a single whale. Meanwhile, the other two members helped us solve the problem.

The bubble was arranged. Milo and Marino moved ahead and slowly touched the water where I fell. They felt the same as what I had been thinking. Marino said there is a huge invisible wall there and the reason our carriage was damaged.

Cali came towards me and we sat near the wall on outdoor chairs. We both touched the invisible wall again and felt a different feeling - one we have never felt in our lives. Cali said, 'Princess, I have never seen or dreamed of such a thing before. I touched the water itself, but my hand is not penetrating beyond this point.'

I said, 'Cali have seen a wall or whatever is allowing the water animals to flow through. Water is moving from this side to the other side and vice versa. My observation is that this wall here was arranged to block only humans and their accessories from passing by.'

Cali said, 'Yes, Princess, what you say is right. Only water and water animals are able to pass through it; that is the reason our whales passed and the carriage couldn't. The belts are broken and the whales were freed up, they went ahead and our carriage was damaged badly.'

I called upon Milo and Marino to think of a solution. Milo said, 'This type of arrangement was not there when I came to your kingdom. I believe this is a protection arranged by the kidnapers to thwart rescuing my father.'

I placed my hand on Marino's shoulder and said, 'Yes, my dear Prince, this is created by them for their protection, which means they are here inside this barrier. We will definitely pass through it but don't yet know how. We have to figure it out.

Milo came up with a plan. 'Princess, I will take a whale and sit on it to pass this wall.' I nodded as an indication of approval. Soon he took a whale that had been driving the second carriage. He sat on it and started moving towards the wall. He look towards us and waved his right hand, smiling at his brilliant idea.

He approached the wall and the whale just entered it. He looked so excited and happy about the success of his idea. The whale's head passed into it. His turn came, but suddenly he fell from the whale and attached to the invisible wall. The whale went into the wall while he remained outside of it.

He came to us and said, 'Sorry Princess, my idea didn't work after all.'

I said, 'Don't worry; at least you tried a solution to the wall problem. The thing is, out of eight whales we are left with three now and only one carriage. From now on, act smart and don't waste our resources.'

It was afternoon and we hadn't found the solution to enter the invisible wall. The two persons who went to check the perimeter returned and said, 'Princess, we have gone a very far distance and found that this invisible wall is around the Tritas kingdom. It is deep into the ocean even the ocean bed.

From our findings, we understood that we cannot go inside this wall from the sides or up and down. It was all around the Tritas kingdom. Water was flowing normally and the animals could move as usual through this wall.

I said, 'Thank you very much for the information. Go and look around. We will figure out the solution.' Marino stood and said, 'Adira, I have an idea: Cali and I have shields on us so, we try to pass like water animals. If not, we forcefully try to break it with our javelins or with our body shields.'

I was about to speak but Cali replied, 'Prince Marino, yes, I understand the idea, but you need not go there for the trial. I will take Milo as my assistant and try it myself.'

Cali stood up. I nodded to move forward. Both Cali and Milo went outside the bubble. She stood far from the wall. She took her javelin, held it firmly, and ran towards the wall very fast. She threw it fiercely and it hit the invisible wall. Everyone looked at the javelin but it was of no use. Its point became like a ball and fell there. Cali saw me and ran superfast. She tried to hit it with her left shoulder. The invisible wall was much stronger than the shield and only a dent formed on the wall. It automatically became normal very soon.

They both came inside the bubble and sat next to me. I said, 'Don't worry, Cali, you have given it a try and we will make it through, definitely. Now I'm hungry so please make a delicious dish for me like yesterday, and we will find the solution after our lunch.

Cali and Milo went into the carriage and soon brought us the requested dish. We all had our lunch, and this time no one spoke a word since they had already implemented their idea, which was of no use. I want to cheer them up, so I said, 'Don't worry, dear friends, there will be a way to cross the wall. We will find it very soon. Forget about the wall and transfer the most important things and gems to the other carriage from the damaged one.'

As all of them were busy transferring things, Marino and I went for a walk outside the bubble. I had some questions about what we would do after going to Tritas? 'Whom shall we question? Do you have anything in mind regarding this?'

Marino said, 'I am so confused and unable to think right now, so I can't answer your question. We, humans, have many restrictions. Just look at those water animals and how freely they can move in the Ocean while happily playing with each other.'

With that observation, I got an idea and shouted and hugged him. He was confused and asked me what was happening. I said, 'I think I found a solution. Let's go inside the bubble, and I will explain my idea to everyone.'

We both went inside and called for everyone to convene. I said, 'Listen carefully, everyone, I have a solution to cross the invisible wall.' Cali asked curiously, 'What is it, Princess?' I started explaining my idea. 'Look around you; all the water animals and even water is moving normally. Only humans and the things made by us are filtered out.'

Milo said, 'Yes, Princess, we can observe it from here.' I interrupted him and said, 'Here is where our answer lies, my dear Milo. My plan is to use one of the most powerful gems and make one whale a very big one, large enough to swallow our carriage easily. This huge whale will cross the invisible wall easily.'

Everyone's faces glowed like stars. They were smiling and clapping.

'This is just an idea and we don't know whether it will work or not. We should feel happy only when we find King Tritan. Okay, I will make the whale bigger and you complete the transfer of our luggage.'

I moved towards a whale a little distance away from our carriage and took out the gem acquired from mount kea. I placed it in my hand and prayed for the Ocean God to make this whale a huge one so the bigger carriage can be swallowed. I looked at the whale and was amazed by its size.

Cali came to me and said, 'We all are ready, my dear Princess. The remaining whales and small carriages are in their respective positions.

I placed my hand on the giant whale's head without speaking a word. It understood everything and opened its giant mouth for us to enter our carriage. The giant whale closed its mouth and started moving towards the wall. We could not see anything outside but expected that we had crossed it. Cali got down from the carriage and stood inside the mouth of the whale, shouting at the whale to stop. It stopped, opened its mouth and we got out. We turned back and saw that we had crossed the wall. We jumped for joy.

Cali said, 'Princess, your plan worked. We are now on the other side of the wall and very near to Tritas kingdom. By evening we will reach it.'

I said in response, 'We still don't know how many traps are in our path. So, be very cautious.' I took the gem out to make the whale small again, but Marino stopped me and requested it remains big. He said, 'I will take care of it in our kingdom as is.

I blinked and returned the gem to my pocket. We entered the carriage and moved forward; the giant whale followed us. Milo asked, 'Princess, now we need ideas to get to our destination.'

I replied, 'If we work for the greater good of the world, God will be with us. He will take care of everything in our path and lead us to success. Milo clapped and soon something strange happened. As Cali was handling the carriage, she called upon me to show me something from the front window. I was shocked.

Milo and Marino also looked while sitting in their respective places. Cali said, 'What shall we do, Princess? An underwater tornado is upon us. It is very huge and fast, which we have never seen.'

Marino said, 'Since we know how to handle tornados, it should be easy to manage. Look everyone, we have seen many tornados and twisters in the past, but this one is very different, so violent and huge. As far as possible, we will try to avoid it, but hold onto something and get ready for impact.'

Milo offered, 'It doesn't look like a normal tornado because it is bending towards objects and pulling them into it. Sit down and hold tight. We are very near.'

The carriage started vibration. we were in the vicinity of the tornado but Cali was trying to bypass it. Nevertheless, it was pulling us strongly. Finally, the tornado took us; we were rotating inside it. Everyone inside the cabin tried their best to be calm and strong, but soon our mental strength was diminished by the tornado's twisting power. We are going underground unlike regular tornados where we would be thrown about. Except for Milo, we were trying to hold onto something. He started acting strange.

None of the others observed this except me. He slowly moved into a small carriage and hid. Soon our large carriage was sucked into the ground by some force. Everyone fell unconscious, and after some time, I woke and looked around. I was locked in a cell probably underground. Each one of us was locked in a separate cell. Two guards were in a hallway. I sat in one corner of the cell and called Cali and Marino through our intercom gems.

Cali's earrings and Marino's wristband vibrated as a result. They came into consciousness and slowly understood the situation, I said to them, 'Friends, don't panic, I believe we are in an underground detention facility, perhaps temporarily created. Everyone is individually locked in different cells. Only two guards are protecting this facility. Think about our escape plan and be strong.'

It was now evening, and the two guards were in the hallway as usual. Our gems were not glowing. My only hope was Milo because he was not in the main cabin when the carriage moved inside from the tornado. As my instinct came true. I heard sounds from outside and saw Milo fighting with the guards. Milo and the guards were fighting with regular javelins. They fought for more than fifteen minutes before one guard went down.

Now Milo started fighting more aggressively with the other guard. He was able to conquer him, so he tied them together. He came towards me and said, 'Sorry, Princess, for the delay in rescuing you. I just got up and saw our situation. I observed their routine and attacked them.'

He opened the cell for me and I said, 'Don't feel sorry about it, Milo, you did the right thing at the right time. I am proud of you and our army of Aqualean.'

We opened the cells for Cali and Marino and four assistants of Marino. I ordered Milo and all the assistants to check the facility thoroughly for security issues and for any leads. When Milo was about to move, Marino said, 'Sorry, Milo, I thought you had left us behind, but now I understood you had a backup plan. I am proud to be part of this team, so thank you.'

Everyone started searching the whole facility but nothing was found. Milo also searched the security and found nothing. But he noticed something very important: the tattoo of the alligator encircled in a ring with a gem on the top of the right-hand wrist. There were sleeping guards as well.

I said, 'It's okay, Milo, we shall move forward. if they wake up, they will not have much information because either they are hypnotized or they had received instructions from a third party, not in the know.

Cali suggested, 'Princess, my instincts say that they have implanted many more tornados around the Tritas kingdom. It will be very difficult to cross without getting trapped. Moreover, our main carriage has been damaged and only a couple of small carriages are left behind with no whales to pull them. So, we have to find an alternative route to our destination.'

'Yes, Cali what you say is true. We cannot proceed on the same path as we planned previously. We shall do something else; let me think of an alternate plan. Meanwhile, take the necessary things from the cabins and be prepared for anything.'

I started pacing about, thinking about how to reach our destination safely and at a faster pace. Cali, watching me, said, 'Princess, why are we just walking? We should plan something.'

Those words struck an idea and I replied, 'Thank you, Cali, for your help. I have an idea of how to move ahead, but it'll be a little slow process.

Cali said, 'It's okay to go slowly. What is the idea, Princess.'

I said to the group, 'Come on, everyone listen carefully. We cannot go through the Ocean waters as it is not safe. My idea is that we go to the Tritas kingdom through an underground tunnel.'

Marino was surprised and asked me, 'Adira, how do you know there is a tunnel from here to Tritas.' I smiled and said, 'Marino, we have to make one as I don't know of any existing tunnel.'

Cali clapped followed by the remaining members of the team. I said, 'We will celebrate after the successful completion of the mission; for now, we have to move forward. My dear friends, we still do not know the direction to start our journey because our equipment is barely working.'

Marino asked me, 'Adira, how come you contacted us through these gems.' I am about to reply when suddenly Cali interrupted me, 'Prince Marino, as we all know, gems have powers sourced from the Ocean. When required, our communication system works directly with less power. After all, these devices are not far apart so it worked. Our icy screen and other gems are not working because this special facility runs on gem-free power.'

Marino said, 'Thank you, Cali, for your insightful words. Now I understand clearly why the gems are not working.' I ordered Milo and the remaining four assistants to make a hole in the wall so the Ocean sand would be visible.

We handed over the three javelins acquired from the village of Calaris to Milo. After ten minutes, he had made a small hole and sand came into the underground chamber. Milo called for me to look and see if the hole was sufficient. I moved towards the hole to have a look. My gem started to glow. It got its powers back. I turned to Milo and said, 'Now I need not answer your question, as my gems will answer it.'

He smiled and ordered the assistants to stay back. I called upon Marino and Cali and said, 'My, dear friends, now we have all the powers of our gems and icy screen.'

I saw on the icy screen the direction of the Tritas kingdom; the screen showed the opposite side of the wall we had perforated. I said, 'We have to move to the other side. The approximate distance is almost eleven miles from here. I will make a tunnel using the javelin and the two gems fixed on it. Everyone, please follow me.'

I placed the javelin horizontally and prayed for the Ocean God to make a path for us to reach our destination. It started to walk towards the wall. It broke and opened a circular passage for us. As we were moving forward, the tunnel was forming. We walked for three to four hours.

I took out my icy screen and located the palace. Fortunately, we were very near to it. We observed many roots. I asked Marino to identify the location. He replied, 'Adira, these roots are the trees in the park within the palace compound, so have reached Tritas.' All the members of the team were excited to have reached our destination. I wanted to go to the surface. We climbed some steps made by my gems and find an old man sitting on a bench under a tree, thinking deeply. Soon Marino called him Grand Advisor and ran to hug him firmly.

Tears drained from the Grand Advisor's eyes, who then said, 'I am very sorry, Prince Marino, many unfortunate things have happened here and we still have no clue about it.' He reacted and took us to an official secret meeting chamber in Tritas. He also said, 'Prince Marino and friends, stay here tonight. Tomorrow morning we will decide how to move forward. Until then, don't leave this room, I will arrange the required things and also inform your mother about you. I will be back in a couple of minutes. Until then please relax.'

The Grand Advisor went outside and came very fast. He said, 'Princes Marino, I cannot trust anyone, but I have a few loyal servants. I have instructed them to inform your mother to come here and also arrange food and comforts for your stay.'

We all settled in and Marino said, 'Please be seated, grand Advisor. I will introduce the remaining members of the team to you. She is Adira, Princess of Aqualean, he is Milo, royal security head of Aqualean, and she is Cali, the best friend of Princess Adira and me, of course. These are the four members from Tritas.'

The Grand Advisor greeted everyone with a smile and said, 'It is good to see you all, but bad in these tough times.'

I replied, 'We are here to help bring back King Tritan, so we have some questions for you; according to inputs given by you, we will plan our strategy accordingly.'

The Grand Advisor said, 'I am always ready to help and take part in this rescue mission. I will give you as much information as possible from my side, so go ahead Princess with your plans.'

I asked him, 'Please explain in detail what happened on the day of the disappearance of the king, any suspects from your perspective, and the rescue measures you have taken to bring him back.'

He replied, 'Princess Adira, on that day, three of us were walking in the corridor – the security head with our beloved king and me. We are walking from one building to another as per our daily routine. Suddenly, he disappeared; there was no sign of him. We didn't hear any sounds. At the same time, I noticed our bubble was shrinking. I ran into the sacred secret chamber and found that the protection gem was missing from its pedestal. I replaced it with a new one and stabilized the bubble. I came out and joined our security head in searching for our king. There are two possible versions to explain his disappearance.'

'The firstborn is for the throne. If Prince Marino had gone missing for a long time, the throne automatically goes to Prince Marino's cousin, the royal minister and one of the king's advisors. He is five years elder than Prince Marino. The second option is that this act was influenced by the evil alligator to secure more gems since we have a gem forest under Tritas' control. Definitely, an insider is involved in our king's disappearance.'

'The last point is that we have sent out forces in all directions. We searched everywhere in the palace. Moreover, we have sent letters to all our allies and nearby kingdoms for help, but until now, we have received nothing. This is all I know, my dear Princess Adira.'

I turned towards him and said, 'Thank you very much, grand Advisor. Starting tomorrow, our action plan is to announce that Prince Marino is the acting king of Tritas until we find his father.'

As I was speaking, the door opened and Prince Marino's mother entered the room. I already know her from my childhood and felt bad about her condition. She hugged Marino and cried. She said, 'My dear Marino, it is good that you weren't here at the time of the disappearance; otherwise you would also be missing. By the Ocean God's grace, you are here with me.

Marino and I tried to calm her. I assured her that I would definitely bring back her husband and soon. She relaxed and Cali said, 'Queen, please don't speak to anyone about our arrival or any information regarding this incident.'

I said, 'Queen, please go to your room and get some rest. Tomorrow morning Marino will be the acting King for the time being. She started walking towards the door and turned back to see Marino. She wiped her tears with her right-hand forefinger and then moved on to her room in the palace.

Cali asked the Grand Advisor, 'Please suggest the best safe and secure place to be in the palace. We want privacy and our plan of action should not be leaked to anyone.'

He replied, 'My dear Cali, I know about this situation. This room is very safe and secure and no information can be leaked from it. This room is designed such that special gems are interlinked through the special gold and silver alloy. These gems are sourced from the gem forest with utmost care as these are very scarce.'

I asked the Grand Advisor one more time, 'Can you suggest any place to search for the King?' He answered, 'Princess, I personally suggest you search the gem forest and also the infinite place near our kingdom. One more thing is that they are in the opposite direction. One is in the northeast corner and the other one is in the northwest corner of the Tritas kingdom. I prefer you start with the gem forest.'

'Yes, Grand Advisor. I would like to start with the gem forest. Tomorrow morning we will start our journey. Now our team includes Cali, Milo, Marino's cousin Alton, your royal security head and me.

The Grand Advisor informed me, 'His name is Brooklyn, Princess. Yes, we will all go together and investigate the origin of this long suspense story.

Marino said, 'Adira, you forgot my name as part of the new team.'

I smiled and said, 'I haven't forgotten you, my dear Prince Marino. From tomorrow, you will be the new King of Tritas. So, look after the royal matters in the kingdom as we will soon be back and let you know everything in detail.'

The grand Advisor concurred and said, 'Yes Prince Marino, you have many issues to address.'

Marino reluctantly accepted my proposal and said, 'Whether I am part of the team or not doesn't matter much to me, the only concern is to bring back my father.'

I said, 'I can understand your pain, my dear. We will bring back your father soon. One more thing I need to inform everyone about is that the details of our mission should not be shared with anyone, even the two new members, Alton and Brooklyn. They will be informed just before we start our journey.'

The Grand Advisor told us to get some rest and that we would meet tomorrow morning. He advised me to never come out unless instructed by him. Everyone nodded their heads, and as we were all tired, we slept right away. Meanwhile, Milo instructed Marino's assistants to take care of room security in shifts. We slept in deeply and rose rejuvenated. We awoke with all sounds that indicated the ceremony for the new King Marino. The Grand Advisor along with Marino's mother entered the room and wished everyone well.

He guided us outside the room and took Marino to make him ready to be King. We were given guest rooms with full security. Within no time, we all met each other in the court hall, waiting for the new King's arrival. Every one of us stood for Marino's arrival in a king's attire. He looked very handsome. In fact, we could not remove our eyes off him. As he entered the hall, all the citizens of the kingdom clapped and shouted, 'Hail, King Marino! Hail King Marino!

He slowly walked toward the throne and stood in front of it. His mother stood next to him, wiping his tears. She was very glad that her son was the new King of Tritas. Nonetheless, her husband was not with them on this auspicious occasion. The Grand Advisor moved toward Marino while an assistant brought in a crown placed in a tray. The crown was studded with diamonds and red and green gems. I had never seen such a beautiful crown in my life. The stones were vibrant and shining like stars. The grand Advisor took the crown into his hands from the tray and Marino bent toward him. He duly placed the crown on Marino's head.

All the persons in the hall clapped and hailed their new King. He slowly moved back and sat on the throne. He looked around the court hall. I also looked at him. I was astonished by the beauty of the hall. It is more beautiful than our hall because of the gems. After all, they have a gem forest nearby so they can be sourced easily as compared to Aqualean. The gems were arranged artistically on the pillars, doors, and windows. It was like heaven. I was in a trance when suddenly everyone stopped hailing the King and the hall was filled with silence

I checked to see what had happened. The King of Tritas waved his hand to everyone and started his first speech as King to his people. I am listening keenly. 'My dear fellow citizens of Tritas, I promise on the Ocean God that I will take care of the well-being of our kingdom and bring back my father while making sure that all the people in our kingdom are safe and secure. Recently I have learned many new things from the kingdom Aqualean and their Princess Adira. I will make our kingdom safe from evil creatures like the alligator and any other threats. I will make this kingdom future ready in all aspects.'

All the people in the hall including me clapped at those words, and we went to our chambers. Cali and I started following him; even Milo also ran behind us. I appreciated Marino's wonderful and inspiring words. The Grand Advisor also came, so I asked that Alton and Brooklyn come as well.

He replied, 'Yes Princess, I have informed the guards to pass the information on that the King wants them here immediately.'

I said to everyone not to reveal any information unless it was relevant to the situation. All the persons in the room nodded their heads. A knocking sound was heard. I blinked my eyes as an indication to let them enter. Both of them entered the room: Alton looked similar to Marino although his hair and eyes were distinct. Brooklyn was six feet tall and very stubborn. I showed my hand to take their seats. They sat opposite me and said nothing.

I asked Alton, 'Do you know anything regarding the missing King Tritas.' He nodded his head that he didn't. I then turned towards Brooklyn and he started saying, 'He disappeared suddenly while we were walking in the corridors here in the palace. We have searched all over in and around the palaces to see if he might be there. The Grand Advisor had gone to the sacred secret chamber with the Queen and said nothing useful was found there. From then on, we were continuously searching the Ocean for him but it ended in vain. Now a little hope of ray has come to our kingdom with you, Princess.'

THREE

GEM FOREST

Okay now, let's not waste our time. we shall move to the gem forest now. Alton was shocked by my decision but no reaction on Brooklyn's face. We took four of Marino's assistants with us and proceeded towards the carriage. Now a total of nine members were on our team. We got into a carriage similar to the one we used to come here unlike the two carriages we had in our original large carriage.

As usual, Cali took the reins. She turned back and asked, 'Is everyone ready for the ride?' All of us at one time said, yes. She pulled the reins and our journey started on a good note.

I asked Alton how much time it would take to reach the forest. 'Yes, Princess, I have been there many times with my uncle and by midday, we will be there. The forest is very huge and only royal family members are allowed to enter safely without security. Others can also enter but it is not preferred unless very necessary. Every time Uncle Tritan and I would go there. our security was left behind at the entrance. After entering, we forget the time while luxuriating in the natural beauty and wonder.'

I asked him to please explain it in detail. He said, 'Princess, I can explain, but as we are going there now itself so please look for yourself and enjoy. Unlike yesterday's journey, today, we didn't face any hurdles. Finally, we were at the entrance of the forest – the most hyped place ever. Everyone got down one by one. Everyone notices that the beautiful entrance was made of roots decorated with leaves and gems.

Alton said, 'Although we can enter from any side as there are no boundaries or fencing, we regularly enter through this root arch. Generally, our security persons stay here, but now we shall do whatever you say.'

'Okay, fine Alton. Except for Marino's four assistants, we all shall go inside the forest.' As per my order, the four assistants stood outside the forest while the remaining persons began entering it. From the first step inside the forest, I was mesmerized.

We walked about two miles, and the deep forest started. The place was so dark that only lighting from the gems is visible, so we slowed down. Meanwhile, something was pinned to my feet. I bent down and took it into my hand. It was a ripe blueberry. I opened the skin of the berry and was shocked to see a blue sapphire inside as a seed. Except Alton, everyone bent down and took berries. Everyone has a beautiful blue sapphire now.

Alton said, 'My dear Princess, not only blue sapphires exist here but each tree has a different fruit - I mean gem. He showed us trees bearing different fruits with different colored gems inside. Trees had any one of these: red gems, green gems, yellow gems, and many more gems never seen before.

Cali asked Alton how diamonds are sourced from here. He replied, 'Cali that is the sad part. Every tree in this forest has many fruits and eventually gems, but coming to the diamonds all the trees have only one diamond in them.

Each tree will have a diamond in its trunk and have to source diamonds only after the completion of the life of the tree. The other end of the forest is cut down for diamonds by unknown persons, and we believe that they are the allies of the evil alligator.

'King Tritan tried very hard to find the solution to this problem but couldn't solve it,' I said, 'Don't worry, Alton, we will find a solution and regrow all the trees that are cut down. Every problem will have a solution; we just must have patience.'

All of a sudden it became very dark. I had been taken somewhere deep. After some time, I realized that every one of them faced a similar experience but their hands and feet were bound.

Suddenly the deep darkness was pierced with bright light. We had been taken by someone underground. Except for Alton and me, all the other people were tied with roots and the room was full of mud.

I shouted, 'Anybody there? Please come forward and we will talk and solve the issues. Then suddenly, a hard and gigantic voice was heard and the front part of the room vibrated heavily. A huge root came out and started talking to me.

'Why are you here? What do you want from here?', said that root. I moved a little forward and said, 'I am Adira, the Princess of Aqualean. We are all here on a rescue mission to find the King of Tritas: Tritan. Can you please help us with our mission?

'Oh! I feel sorrowful after hearing those words from you. He is the protector of this gem forest. Usually, only people with royal blood enter this forest. We can sense the person with royal blood. That is the reason you both have been left free and the rest others are tied.

I said, 'We are not here to disturb your customs; as I said we are on a rescue mission. So, please set them free and guide us to King Tritan. One more thing: do you have a name?

A beautiful woman appeared before us and spoke to me, 'Princess, my name is Aspen. I am the Queen of this forest and the trees. We have certain powers for each tree, but for a limited range and not out of the forest. It is mostly used for our own protection,' said the Queen.

'Queen Aspen can you please find the King with your powers,' I asked her. She smiled at me and said, 'Definitely.' She waved a root in the air and suddenly many roots came out of the ground and took me to a separate room.

The queen started the conversation with me and said, 'Princess, I want you to help with one major issue - to save this forest for future generations.e is He

A group of people is coming to take all the gems from the ripe fruits and even the unripe fruits. It is one thing to do that, but they are also cutting down the trees for the diamonds from each tree trunk.

I said, 'Queen Aspen, you said each one has different powers, so why don't you defend yourselves and get rid of those thieves?

She replied, 'Princess, we do have powers, but as I said it is limited to this forest area. Also, we don't have deadly powers to defend ourselves. They made a shield with our gems and diamonds to use against us. They go on cutting down the trees at least twice weekly. One more thing is that the King of Tritas is the protector of this forest, and it is our duty to help you people in this mission. We have spoken about many things and strategies for the mission.'

Queen Aspen guided me towards the gem thieves' den and urged my help to catch them and hand them over to her. She gave me the most powerful diamond and a green gem to help us in finding and capture them. When we were done, the Queen took me to the room where my other team members were waiting. Cali eagerly asked me what had happened. I replied, 'I have a little more information regarding our mission. Now we have a new mini-mission to look after very urgently.'

'Will you explain it or leave us in suspense?' I replied, 'Yes, my dear Cali, I will explain everything during our journey toward our mini mission.

'What mini mission? You are hiding something from me,' said, Cali. I just smiled and said, 'Okay, friends, let's move. Now we are on a new mission. So are you with me?' Everyone replied in a single voice, yes!

I blinked at Queen Aspen and she smiled back. It made our room dark. In the blink of an eye, we were out at the root arch at the entrance of the forest. I said, 'Everyone inside the carriage. Be alert and obey my orders carefully.'

All the team members nodded their heads. I said, 'Cali, take the carriage to the other side of the forest.' After this statement, I observed everyone's expressions keenly and none of them reacted except for two people: Alton and Brooklyn.

Generally, this would be normal because the two belonged to Tritas. They were in the palace with the King when he went missing. Alton asked me, 'Princess, why are we now going there? Do you have information that King Tritan is there? As far as I know, there are many gem thieves on the other side of the forest. So we should be careful while dealing with them.'

Soon Brooklyn said, 'Yes, Princess, what Alton said is absolutely right. I believe we are wasting our time deviating from our main mission. So, please consider your decision. Our priority is our King Tritan and we can deal with them later.'

'Thank you for your suggestions. I have made a final decision. We are going there since this will help us in finding King Tritan. Cali was driving very fast but the journey could take last a couple of hours.

One thing I understood is definitely that these two persons, Alton and Brooklyn, know something about this missing issue. I have to dig deep and find out the mystery in all this. Finally, we were at the other side of the gem forest and Cali stopped the carriage, and we got down. After getting down, I looked around and was shocked because there were no trees in the visible areas. It looked to be a very bad situation. The trunks were cut vertically, ostensibly for the diamonds in them.

I looked towards Brooklyn and asked, 'What is this and what are you doing for the protection? I think you have done nothing to protect the forest and allow the thieves to collect the precious gems and diamonds. I believe there is a definite connection between this deforestation and the missing King Tritan.'

Alton and Brooklyn kept their heads down and did not react. I said, 'There is no use for your sorrow and regret. You didn't act in time. It's okay as nothing is too late. At least we are here to take action. Come on, everyone, let's look for clues any signs of the persons involved.' Cali and I moved in one direction. All the other team members were divided into two-member teams to look in all directions for clues.

We slowly walked in the opposite direction; around half a mile from there, we observed some marks on the Ocean bed. I called Cali to take a closer look at them. She observed closely and came to the conclusion that the marks were the alligator's sled. There were also alligator body marks on the ground. I understood that all the things that were happening were backed by the alligator and he is sourcing all the gems from the forest and the kingdoms. He was planning something very big. We had to figure it out before he become too dangerous and powerful.

After an hour, we all gathered at the carriage. I asked everyone what they found. The common answer I got was that many people - at least fifteen to twenty - are coming for the gems regularly. We moved towards the thief's den, which was away from the forest but very near - maybe a ten-to-fifteen minutes journey. We found their den and stooped our carriage a little away from it. We got down from the carriage and started walking towards their hiding place.

Drawing near the hiding place, I was a bit shocked to see a kind of mini palace made only of wood with no sign of gem decoration on it. Maybe because the gems were transported from here to the alligator's den.

I signaled everyone to hide behind the walls and wait to attack until my orders. Cali, Milo and I moved forward and stood behind the entrance of the main hall. From there, we could clearly hear their voices.

One of the thieves was talking to other thieves, 'My dear friends, from today forward, we have to increase our gem collection as per orders received from the high command. We also have to develop new weapons from these gems. We may encounter some protests from the forest and from the kingdom of Tritas. We have information that someone is helping from the Aqualean kingdom. So be careful and watch each other while in the forest.

By listening to them, I understood that they were talking about us. I peeked into the room through the window and was surprised to see inside the hideout heaps of gems segregated according to color and size, all made ready for transportation.

I signaled my team members outside the wall to join us. Now we were standing near the main door, our javelins pointing at them. I said, 'Everyone freeze. Your game is over now. By the way, I am Adira, the Princess of Aqualean here to capture you and save the forest.

No one moved, but I could see from their faces that they weren't even afraid. So I wanted to show them an example. I took the blue sapphire my father had presented to me and closed my eyes. I asked something they could never have imagined. I placed the gem in my pocket and soon a miracle happened. Gems from the nearest heap joined together to form a cage and captured one person from their group. The thieves were shocked.

I then asked Cali and Milo to sweep the complete building and look for any persons or clues. I turned towards the one I assumed was their leader and said, 'You must surrender to us; otherwise you will regret it later. You have taken the wrong road by choosing to fight us.

He laughed and said, 'We have seen such people as your group. We will captivate you and use you as leverage to secure precious gems from Aqualean as well as Tritas.' Meanwhile, Cali and Milo came to where we stood and said that nothing was found in the rooms. Everywhere only heaps of gems and packed gems for transportation.'

Soon they revolted, took their javelins and started throwing gems at us. As they had long been dealing with gems. they knew what type to use to defeat the enemy. The gems slowly radiated a heat we could not tolerate so we left immediately. They also came out and used the same strategy, throwing heat radiating gems at us. But I had an idea of how to tackle the heat. I took a gem given to me by Queen Aspen and prayed for a solution. Every person on our team should have a gem over their head with water continuously flowing all over their body.

As per my request, our team members were under a waterfall. So the heat generated by their gems didn't affect us. Their team leader got angry and acted accordingly. He took a power gem and threw it in front of me to my surprise. As I had fought with the alligator recently, this time I clearly understood that something was going to happen. My curiosity ended very fast, and the gem lying on the floor attracted many others from the heap to join together to make balls that fit in a palm.

These balls were all over, rolling on the ground. We are unable to move, but one of Marino's assistants moved a little and fell on the ground. He couldn't get up. Their leader was laughing at us and said, 'I thought you were so powerful and intelligent, but I cannot see such qualities in you.'

Milo shouted at him and said, 'Keep your tongue in control. She is the Princess of Aqualean. How dare you speak like that. I will see your end.' I turned towards Milo and said, 'Milo, there is no use castigating them. We have to make our final move now and capture them.'

Every member of the thieves' team took a gem and said after their leader, 'Oh, lord alligator, make a chamber of gems to block us from the enemy. Many gems from all the heaps moved towards us and formed a large room to hamper us. All the members were encapsulated in that large room. Milo threw his javelin at one of the walls with the intention of breaking it, but his attempt went in vain. I heard their leader again laughing at us. I understood that he wouldn't stop there as he wanted us to suffer more.

The walls moved towards us, making the room smaller and smaller. We felt strong and confident that we would get through this. Now Cali tried with her own javelin with a special gem on it. It didn't work. The room was reducing continuously. Everyone's facial expression changed to fear. Only Cali and I knew that we would definitely prevail. I called Cali to come towards me and said, 'Hold my hand and take the powerful gems there with you.

We both caught a handful of gems and prayed, 'Oh, Ocean God and Queen of the forest, please make a tunnel under our feet and let us escape from here.' We opened our eyes and all the gems given to us by the forest queen disappeared. Only the two powerful gems - one my father gave me and one I brought from the mountain - remained in my hand.

Soon a tunnel formed under our feet and we escaped. Now we were exactly below the hideout. Slowly, I made the steps toward the living room. I climbed in first, and the remaining team members followed me. The thieves were standing outside the building, laughing at us while thinking we were still inside that shrinking room.

Everyone on our team came out and I signaled them not to make any sounds. I took my javelin, climbed the diamond heap, and stood on it. I wished the gems to tie their hands and legs, then connect all of them with a diamond rope. The thieves tried to escape. One said to me, 'Why are you here? You should be inside the shrinking room, right? I smiled and said, 'I am Adira the Princess of Aqualean.'

The thieves were now tied to our carriage back, and we rode towards the forest. When almost near the forest, we heard some sounds. A new hurdle must be welcoming us. Cali looked out and said, 'Princess, the forest is welcoming us with a gem rain. We stopped the carriage at the back entrance of the forest near the deforestation area. Queen Aspen came from the roots of the trees and started walking towards me. Her face was glowing like the moon. She seemed very glad that the thieves had been captured and brought to her.

She waved her hand and the roots from the ground arose fiercely and took all the thieves into the underground. Soon Brooklyn reacted and asked the queen, 'What will you do with them.' She replied, 'Look son, these people come here almost every day with protection to collect gems and diamonds from the young trees by cutting them down. I was very worried about the forest until now. Princess Adira solved the problem of deforestation and helped restore balance to the Ocean.' She presented every one of us with precious gems and gave each a special diamond that didn't disappear. Their power would never be lost.

She thanked me and my team members once again for helping to save the gem forest. She again took me to a secret chamber and said to me personally, 'Now I believe my full powers are back and I can give you information about the missing King.

I was very eager to know about him, so I said, 'Yes, Queen, please tell me. It will be very helpful for our mission.' She started saying, 'Adira, after going missing, King Tritan was not brought here. As you said, he is unable to track on the icy screen or any other tracking devices, but don't worry, my dear. He is still alive. I don't know the exact location, but I can suggest some possible hideouts.

'The first one was the infinite palace built by the ancestors of the Tritas kingdom. The second one was the invisible bubble area. Both were dangerous, but the second one was much more dangerous. So be careful. The person

I suspect by instinct will be a person on your team. Handle him carefully; he may be doing this for power, money, or some personal hidden motive.

Now I can co-relate the places that the forest Queen suggested with the book that I have brought with me from Aqualean. It also explains the same places. So, I have to concentrate on those areas.

From the Queen's suggestions, I suspect Marino's cousin as the culprit. The Queen blessed us all. We bade farewell to her and started our journey to Tritas.

FOUR

INFINITE PALACE

This time, I felt like we had reached Tritas faster. We met the Grand Advisor personally. Cali was with me and the Grand Advisor sent the message to the King that we are home. Soon Marino came in hurriedly, hugged me, and cried, 'Adira, what happened? Any breakthrough on this mission? I am very worried. Next time, I will also come with you, and please don't say no.'

I said, 'Calm down, Marino. Yes, I have lots of information to share with you. First, cool down and sit. I will explain everything in detail.' I explained how we met Queen Aspen and how we fought at the hideout and caught the thieves. I told him that his father's disappearance was half solved now that we know that the main person behind the mystery is the alligator - most probably because his father is the protector of the gem forest.

'I know your next question is when will we start our next trip in this mission. Marino, the Queen suggested two places, the day after tomorrow we shall go to the infinite palace. Don't worry, you are also coming along.

Cali interrupted me and said, 'He is the King of Tritas now and may have many official works. Is it possible to take

King Marino with us? I replied, 'Yes, my dear Cali, it is very much possible. He is also very eager to join us. Moreover, the palace was built by his ancestors so he is very much required to be on this journey. I need to stress that these details must not be shared with anyone, even with Brooklyn and Marino's cousin Alton. I will let you know more later, but as of now, please don't ask me anything.'

'We will start the next search trip day after tomorrow. Get ready for that, Cali, and make sure our carriages are well supplied for our mission.' She nodded her head and said nothing. Marino asked me a question, 'Adira, why the gap of one day? Why can't we go tomorrow?'

'Yes, my dear Marino, I gave one-day break in the mission because I need to gather information for our next trip. I also need to analyze data given to me by the forest queen. I will let you know at the right time. As of now, I can't say much about this mission.'

He responded, 'It's okay, Adira, I will not pressurize you on this issue. You have full freedom. Go get some rest. We will meet later, and I will take you to the countryside of Tritas.' I smiled at him, and he left the room.

Cali and I sat on the couch for some rest. On this mission, rest means sitting and analyzing the data. We were the only ones present. I said to Cali, 'Listen carefully, my dear, and give me suggestions on this complex issue.'

She replied, 'As you wish my dear Princess. I will be on your side till my last breath in this world. Now go ahead.' I opened up and started speaking, 'Cali, the forest Queen took me two times to a secret room and said that the mole may be likely in this kingdom, either Brooklyn or Alton.

We cannot underestimate anyone or take anyone's side. We cannot judge anyone until we find proof in the right manner without affecting Tritas' name and fame.'

She asked me, 'How do we find the correct culprit from those two persons?' With my right hand on my forehead, I said that was the biggest task. 'First, we have to confirm if my analysis is right because the Queen didn't gave their names directly. She only said, 'The culprit is among your team.'

'I have analyzed the persons on our team other than you, me, and Milo. Cali has suggested using our new invention, the secret voice transmitters and location trackers. Then we can easily find the mole. I liked what she suggested and said, 'Fine, Cali, we will go with this plan to find the mole in Tritas.'

Cali said, 'I will take care of arranging for the transmitters on their bodies. They are invisible and very easy to place. Just put them in our hands and turn on the invisible mode. Once we touch the intended body surface, it will attach to their body but they will not feel it. Nobody will know about it. Moreover, it has a very wide range and can be tracked and controlled through the icy screen.

She added, 'Princess, I have arranged a team to collect all the gems from the hideout and bring them back to Tritas along with the thieves. This will be supervised by Milo. I said to Milo to take control of the hideout area and arrange for constant security. 'Good work, Cali, my opinion is the same on this issue. I know you will follow my heart. I am so lucky to have you, Cali.' She smiled and said, I feel the same, my dear Princess: best friends forever.'

We both took some rest and got ready for the next day. I went to talk with Marino in his room while Cali went to meet Brooklyn and Alton to attach the secret tracker. We walked through the corridors of the palace. I sensed an uncountable number of gems, but they were not using them properly for developing defense systems, decorating the palace, expanding the kingdom and the bubble, etc.

We two got separated at a point. When together, I said to Cali, 'Be very careful, my dear, and don't hesitate to contact me if anything is beyond your control.' She nodded and waved her hand before moving ahead to complete the task.

I reached Marino's room and knocked on his door. Soon he opened the door and welcomed me into his room. 'I am very happy to have you, my dear Adira.' I answered, 'I am here to discuss some important information.'

He said, 'Go ahead, I am listening.' As per the details provided by Queen Aspen, Cali and I have come to the conclusion that the culprit may be Alton or Brooklyn. As of now, this is in doubt and we don't have any hard proof. Cali had gone to fix invisible trackers on their bodies. I also need to inform you that Cali has arranged to bring the treasure, I mean the huge pile of gems, and the thieves here to be supervised by Milo. So please relax. Tomorrow morning, we will start from here and according to the Grand Advisor, we may reach our destination by evening.'

'As I promised, I will include you on the team. As for Brooklyn and Alton, I haven't decided what to do. Shall we take them with us or leave them here? What is your opinion?

He replied, ' Adira, my opinion is not to have them with us if they are suspects. They may harm us. It is a very big palace. One more thing I want to ask you is why this indirect inquiry? Shall we take them into custody and make them reveal the truth?'

'No, no, not now. I will tell you what to do next. We just follow them secretly. By now Cali should have finished her work and be on the way back. Soon she entered the room and greeted Marino. She turned towards me and said, 'Princess, I have attached the trackers without their notice.

I believe Alton may be the mole since his behavior is so weird.'

'Okay, let's wait for the results. Don't make any assumptions now.'

Marino said, 'Shall I show the palace to you both; till now, you are confined to one room. Let me show the beauty of Tritas. Cali said, 'I have some work to complete, so please excuse me.'

Marino said okay. 'After your work, Cali, meet us in the dining hall for lunch.' She nodded, bowed and left. I turned towards Marino to ask, 'Do you know why Cali didn't want to come with us now? He replied, 'Yes, my dear, she clearly said she has work to complete.'

I laughed and said, 'No, my dear, she want to give us some privacy, so she left us alone.' He smiled, nodded his head, and caught my right hand with his left one. He said, 'Shall we have a look at the beauty of the Tritas.'

We both started walking in the corridors of the palace. He explained how his ancestors had built it and it hadn't been renovated for centuries. I turned towards him and said, 'It is so beautiful, so why not renovate it to make it the most beautiful Palace without changing the design? At least you haven't decorated it with gems even though you have access to a lot of them.'

He said, 'Look Adira, that is the difference between boys and girls. I have tried many times but didn't propose any ideas for the renovation. I felt it looked good so I dropped the idea.'

I laughed loudly and said, 'Okay, I will be here for some time after finding your father to make this palace a beautiful place. I will construct a new stadium and add some towers to the palace. Let's go into town and find out how the people are living. We can perhaps provide a better existence.

We two roamed around the town till afternoon and then returned to the palace. Cali was waiting for us. She asked what we did outside the palace. I had no reply but we were about to have lunch in the dining hall for the first time since coming to the kingdom of Tritas.

As for the palace, I saw a lot of scope for upgrading to make it more beautiful. I said to Marino, 'I will also keep in mind this dining hall and this table for renovation. He showed me thumbs up and said that we will start our journey from here tomorrow.

'Don't hurry, we will start after breakfast. Cali will look after the arrangements.' Cali stopped eating and nodded. She asked, 'Princess, is Milo accompanying us on this journey?

'By evening, all the gems from the hideout and the thieves will reach the palace. If the work is done, he will be accompanying us, otherwise, we will move forward without him. Bring some extra communication devices, Cali,' I replied to her.

Even though we roamed the palace and the town, we still went back to our secret meeting room. As of now, we three were in that room. Marino was so excited about tomorrow's trip.

Cali stood and said, 'Princess and King Marino, I will go now and look after the arrangements for our eventual travel. I said, 'Be careful, my dear. Take Milo with you if he is here or take Marino's personal guards. Do not contact Alton and Brooklyn on any issues or for any requirements.'

Soon she left the room and after some time, Marino also stood up and said, 'Princess, I will also take leave for today. We shall meet tomorrow. I have a royal meeting this afternoon and later I will be with my mother to soothe her grief and make little happier tonight.

I said, 'I can understand your feelings, Marino. Don't worry, all the problems will come to an end very soon.' He left the room. I took out the gems given to me by Queen Aspen and tested them in different ways. I combined their powers and made many combinations of gem balls so I could get their optimum effect during the battle.

I found many combinations that worked perfectly and I will explain them to Marino and Cali when the time comes. For now, I will get some rest. I slept on the couch and thought about tomorrow's search plan at the infinite palace.

Soon I went into a deep sleep and slept for a couple of hours. I heard a voice, 'Princess, Princess. At first, I thought it was a dream and later realized that Cali has come to the room to wake me up.' I asked for updates.

'Princess, Milo is here. He has completed the work assigned to him. I told him to get ready for tomorrow's journey and to keep his distance from all persons of Tritas. Now he is waiting outside the room for further orders,' said Cali.

I started thinking about how to find King Tritas in the infinite palace. Marino has said that it has infinite floors up and down and is unmanned. I am wondering about how to find him in that huge palace.

Cali, seeing me in deep thought said, 'Don't worry, my dear Princess. I know you will definitely solve the mystery of this palace. Don't think too much about it. Now come on, let's pack our luggage for the two or three-day trip. So your mood can change, you will be in the midst of the mission, and your mind will get some rest.

We all assembled in the dining hall as per our plan. I sat next to Marino and Cali sat opposite me. Marino asked me, 'Is everything ready, Adira? Shall we start after our breakfast?' I was about to answer his question when an assistant came to Marino and said that Brooklyn was waiting outside to meet us.

I said to Marino, 'Let him wait till we finish our breakfast.' We did and I said to everyone to speak in a balanced and diplomatic way when answering his questions. Marino waved his hand to a servant to let him in.

He entered the dining hall and bent to Marino. He said, 'Oh, my lord, I have heard that you are going to the infinite palace today. As I am your chief of security and don't know about it. Am I not coming with you?'

Marino replied, 'Yes, Brooklyn, nothing important on this journey. I just want you to look here in the palace and take care of matters in my absence.' He bowed and said, 'As you wish, my lord. I will take care of this palace and report everything. I showed him thumbs up that he had dealt with the situation aptly.

We three stood and started walking towards our carriage, which was waiting outside the palace. Milo followed us. We reached the carriage to find Marino's four personal assistants waiting for us, they opened and said that all the arrangements were done for our journey.

As usual, Cali took the reins and looked at me for the signal to start. I blinked my eyes. She pulled the reins for a good start. I don't know why, but today I was confident that I would definitely get a lead on King Tritan. We traveled the whole day to reach the palace with a couple of breaks. I alit down and was astonished by the beauty of the palace. It had a large tower and three small towers. It was decorated with pearls all over.

Soon the remaining members in the carriage got down and said in chorus, 'Wow it's beautiful. Cali asked Prince

Marino, 'Prince Marino, I heard that this palace was built by your ancestors a long time ago, but why has it not been put into use? I see that it is not under construction. In fact, it is a finished palace.'

He responded, 'Yes, Cali, what you have heard is true. This is a completed masterpiece built by my ancestors. I have heard many stories from the elders in our kingdom that after the completion of this palace, one day it was opened. On the day of the opening ceremony, a child went into the palace and started walking downstairs. everyone was busy with their work and receiving guests. He went alone and nobody noticed him. He went down and down so deep that he didn't return. Only that evening his parents noticed that their son was missing. Everyone searched a thousand floors up and a thousand floors down, but their search ended in vain.

Nobody found him and so his grandfather declared that the palace should be closed forever to anyone including royal family members. The child who went missing was my great-great-grandfather. So from that day on, this palace is forbidden. After centuries, we are the first people to enter this palace.

'Listen, everyone, don't get too excited and be careful as there are infinite stairs up and infinite stairs going down. Don't go alone. If anyone goes missing, we may find or may not find that person. We shall take some rest and start our search tomorrow morning.

Milo and his assistants arranged tents for use, we had our dinner and sat on a bench. Cali, Marino, and I were talking about tomorrow's plan. I explained that Marino and I would go with a couple of guards and Cali would go with Milo and a couple of guards. Everyone agreed to my proposal. I also said, 'Don't come back in the middle of the day and search for any clues. At the end of the day come back whether or not you found anything. Gathering here is a must for everyone. By the way, try at least one hundred floors in the direction you take.'

Marino and Cali nodded their heads and Marino said, 'We have our communication devices with us so we need not worry. Cali interrupted him and said, 'Prince Marino, they will work on each floor but we are split into two teams heading in opposite directions. That may baffle, gem communication signals so we may or may have communication with the other team.'

I suggested to everyone to go inside assuming we have no communication with the other team. 'As much as possible better, stick with your own team members all the time. If new ideas arise, we shall discuss them tomorrow morning before entering the palace.'

Marino said good night and went to his tent. I then said to Cali, 'My dear, we have to find some clues to the disappearance of the King. I strongly believe that the culprits have come here as a hideout. The best place for them to hide is a palace, which is forbidden for centuries.'

We slowly moved into our tent. I asked Cali about the security during the night and she said that all four members have Milo guarding us. Soon we both fell into a deep sleep. Cali woke a little earlier than me. She placed her hand on me and gently woke me up. I looked towards her, surprised that she was ready for the mission. I got ready very fast and met Marino and Milo at the beautifully carved temporary dining table. We had our delicious breakfast on a pearl design plate.'

As per our plan, we split up into two groups. Marino extended his hand to me to move forward and the remaining members followed. First Marino and I entered the palace and saw the court hall. I was astonished and didn't speak for a minute. I was trying to find the optimal words to describe its beauty. It was very far from what I had imagined. The throne is a crystal clear single large diamond studded with all types of colored stones. We couldn't move our eyes away from it. There were also two huge statues on both sides of the throne that looked natural despite their size.

The pillars were studded with colored gems, forming beautiful creeper vines, climbing the pillar. The windows and doors were studded with diamonds and stones that resembled lotuses. Marino placed his hand on my shoulder and gently shook me. I came back to reality and looked around to see the remaining members in a stupor like me. I moved towards Cali and touched her. She shouted, 'Princess, this is awesome; we shall stay here forever.'

The remaining team members came out of their trance and were very excited by the beauty of the palace. To get acquainted with the palace, everyone looked at each room of the palace on the main floor together. Each room was beautifully decorated and had a unique combination of colors. It was mesmerizing and soothing to our souls. We searched every nook and cranny of the palace's ground floor, but we didn't find any clues.

We returned to the court hall and decided to take two paths as decided yesterday. Cali's team went downstairs and our team remained in the hall. Marino asked me why we were waiting. I said, 'I am thinking about where the cowards could be hiding? We have to find them at any cost. My instinct says today will be a breakthrough for all of us. We will have our answers soon.'

We started walking upstairs enthusiastically. We completed the search of the second floor very fast as it was a replica of the first one. Not a single gem color or item of furniture was different from the ground floor. I went onto a balcony and saw the beauty of the Ocean, the garden, and our tents and carriage visible from there. Marino said, 'Come on, Adira, we have so many rooms to search, and each balcony will be the same.'

We went to the third floor, searched thoroughly, and nothing was found. We searched the fourth floor, fifth floor, and so on until we reached the tenth floor. I stood on a balcony, feeling the same as the one on the first floor. Marino moved towards me and tried to place his hand on my shoulder. I jumped off the balcony. Oddly, it was just one floor above the ground floor from that balcony. We realized that we could not go to any floor through the balcony, only the first floor. Jumping was easy and fun from the tenth floor, but the sad part is I would have to climb all ten floors to reach it.

I climbed all ten floors nonstop. Finally, I reached them, breathing heavily. Marino came and said. 'Do not do such things from higher floors because it will be very difficult to climb all the floors again.'

I nodded my head and didn't speak for some time. We went floor by floor in search of King Tritan. While climbing from the fifty-fifth to the fifty-sixth floor, I said to Marino, 'Hey, actually I jumped from the tenth-floor balcony just to know what was one floor down and also for any clues. Next time, I won't jump from any balcony because I cannot climb all up to these floors again.'

He turned towards me, laughing, and said, 'I can understand, my dear. Climbing all these stairs is a bit of a difficult task.' We took a break on the fifty-sixth floor and had some snacks.

Marino asked me, 'We have searched more than fifty floors. I don't think we will find anything here, Princess.' I said firmly, 'Don't be disappointed, my dear. I have hope that we will get some clues to find your father.'

After some time, we started climbing stair by stair and found nothing. We crossed the hundredth floor and reached the one hundred and seventh floor. Marino said in a low tone, 'We shall go back from here. We are wasting our time searching here. Who would come this high with a kidnapped person?'

I requested, 'Marino, please, we shall search at least a couple of floors more and stop for today. Then we shall go down and find an alternate way to search the palace. If you are not interested or too tired, relax here and I will search those two floors and come back to you.'

He replied, 'Okay, my dear, I will also come with you but only two floors. After that, we shall go to our tents.' I nodded and proceeded toward the one-hundred-and-eighth floor. We searched the floor thoroughly and found nothing. The two assistants and Marino were waiting in the court hall when Marino called me to come back. I went to the bedroom and found nothing visible.

While I was searching, I felt pain in my right leg, something like a pin or stone. I was surprised to see a ring with a beautiful blue sapphire gemstone. I took it in my hand and rushed towards Marino to show it to him. He observed it closely and said, 'It is my father's ring. He started wearing it a while back. Sometimes it glows, but I don't know why.'

We again searched that floor keenly but found nothing. Marino said, 'We shall go down to our tents and analyze this ring.' All four members walked towards the balcony and stood ready to jump. Marino was at the edge, but suddenly, I got an idea and shouted not to jump. I threw a gem to create a ladder to get down. One by one, we got down and moved toward our tents.

We refreshed and waited for Cali's team to come to our resting area. After a couple of hours, they reached the tents and everyone looked exhausted. After a rest, we enjoyed a super tasty finger-licking dinner. Now I asked Cali, 'My dear, how many floors did you covered? Did you find anything related to our search?' She said, 'We covered 369 floors and found nothing. All floors are alike, but no clue of any living being on any floor.'

Our team clapped for their achievement of covering such a huge number of floors. Milo said, 'My dear Princess, it became very easy. We sub-divided into groups and searched each floor alternatively.'

I said, 'Good plan, Cali and Milo. Cali asked me, 'Any update from your side, Princess.' I nodded and said, 'Yes, Cali, we have found a ring that belongs to King Tritan on the one hundred and eighth floor.'

I showed the ring to Cali and she took it into her hand. I saw her tiredness disappear after seeing it. Milo took the ring and observed it closely. He said, 'Princess, I have seen this ring before on our King Tritan. I can definitely say that this ring has powers, but I don't remember what exactly.'

'Don't worry, Milo, we will figure it out soon and take some rest for today.' My confidence level increased after finding the ring. That night I slept after thinking deeply about the solution to searching all the floors without going to each individual one. With that thought, I went into a deep sleep and as usual, the next morning Cali woke me up. We all assembled at the breakfast table. I was still thinking about how to find an optimal solution for this infinite problem.

Everyone began chitchatting about the palace, but I was not interested. I was slowly eating my breakfast when Marino said sadly that we had so many gems and so many advanced gadgets with us but still we were not able to find his father. Suddenly, I stood and shouted, 'I have an idea, my dear friends. Listen carefully, till now we have been searching each floor one by one. It is a hectic task and almost impossible to complete as it is an infinite palace. We can use our icy screen to scan the entire infinite palace and report any abnormalities or differences on each floor.'

Cali asked, 'Princess, we had thought that the icy screen would work only in a finite area, and as it is an infinite palace, how can we use the screen?'

'Yes, my dear Cali, we cannot use the icy screen directly. Here comes my idea. It is very simple. With the help of the power gems, we can encapsulate the entire palace in a bubble so it looks one a single floor from the outside. Now the infinite palace would be in a finite bubble and we use our icy screen to scan for any oddities on each floor.'

All the members stood and clapped non-stop. I said. 'It is just starting idea and for our greater mission, we need to do a lot more. You can clap for me after we find King Tritan.'

As per my idea, I took a powerful gem from my bag and prayed to the forest goddess to create a bubble around the palace. Within no time, the palace was covered with a beautiful transparent bubble. I took the icy screen and placed the same gem on top of it, asking the screen to scan any movement or activity. The screen showed the palace first and that all the floors were alike. I was very happy that my idea had worked and we had cracked the whole infinite palace problem while searching for it in just a couple of minutes.

I asked the screen to scan backward in time for any movement in the palace. The screen started searching from that instant and showed our faces and each and every detail of our movements from yesterday, even if King Tritan was taken from the palace. It went on searching day by day backward. Suddenly, it showed a day when the King and four persons were walking outside the palace. The King had his hands and his eyes were blindfolded. The screen showed past days and stopped where the King was kidnapped.

The king was captured and a four-member team took him to the palace and placed him on the tenth floor and for a couple of days. Then he was moved to the one hundred and ninth floor. They were there for more than ten days. I asked the screen to show the faces of the culprits. It showed all three faces but one was covered with a cloth. The three members were new to us. Marino said, 'I believe they don't belong to the kingdom of Tritas.'

The screen also showed that the King intentionally removed his ring and dropped it before he was moved to another place. I said, 'Look everyone, the king wanted us to find the ring and use it to get to him, so he left for us there.'

We checked with the screen thoroughly at all angles for any clue. We found nothing other than the ring. Finally, we decided to wind it up and go home for further analysis. Cali and Marino, with the help of assistants, packed everything for our return journey. We started to go back home with some small satisfaction that we had a clue about the kidnapping. Soon we would break the mystery and find him with the help of the ring.

Suddenly Milo said, 'Princess, now I remember this ring. I saw it when your father recently met with King Tritan with other delegates. I asked him about the ring, and he replied that it is a tracker that records everything and stores it. I understood that in that meeting, all the kings started to wear the ring for safety and security purposes. With this ring, we can analyze the information, but I don't know how to decode it. I didn't ask your father, the King of Aqualean, much regarding this.'

We discussed options to decode it as we didn't know exactly what to do. Meanwhile, we reached the Tritas kingdom and entered the palace. I instructed everyone not to reveal anything that we found in the Infinite palace. We all dispersed and reached our rooms. I asked Cali to analyze the trackers attached to Brooklyn and Alton. She said, 'Yes my dear Princess, I will be on it.

I heard someone knocking on the door and I gave permission to enter. The Grand Advisor entered the room and I offered him a seat. He thanked me. Then he asked, 'Princess, have you found anything and how many floors did you climb?' I replied, 'We covered one hundred floors upstairs and more than three hundred and fifty floors downstairs, but found nothing. All the floors are alike, so we returned.'

He seemed sad and asked me, 'Exactly hundred floors, Princess? I nodded and left the room. Soon we were sleeping for the night. In the morning, Cali started investigating the trackers she had attached to Brooklyn and Alton with the help of the icy screen.

FIVE

BUBBLES BUBBLE

First, she started tracking Alton's details like where he had been in the past two days and with whom he has been speaking. She took the icy screen and placed a gem on top of it. She started tracking him, but it took a couple of hours. She also completed tracking of Brooklyn.

It was now afternoon and we hadn't moved from our rooms. I asked Cali for an update. She said, 'My dear Princess, I have completed an analysis of both suspects. Shall I explain the details now or later in the evening?'

'I am listening, my dear.' Cali continued, 'First we go with the Alton, the beloved cousin of King Marino. After attaching the tracker to his body, he went to the gem forest and was there for the whole day while we were busy traveling to the infinite palace. Surprisingly, he met Queen Aspen there and spent a half day with her. He asked her about the rare gems and about the powers of each gem as well as their availability. The forest queen answered him gently with elaborate information. He collected some gems from the forest and returned in the evening to the palace.'

'The next day he met the Grand Advisor and also some security guards in the palace. He went out of the palace and met people in town. He gave one gem to a person and returned. I didn't find any suspicious activity over these two days.'

Now comes our royal security head, Brooklyn. The day we were traveling to the infinite palace, I observed suspicious activity. He went to the prison to meet the gem thieves and was with them for a couple of hours. I couldn't hear their discussion. I think they used anti-tracker and anti-transmitter gems so the information was not clear. The next day he was in and around the palace. He met King Marino's mother, the Grand Advisor and some guards. I strongly believe that Brooklyn is involved in the missing conspiracy. Anyway, the tracker is on both their bodies so we will have new information to analyze in the coming days.'

'Yes, my dear Cali, we cannot conclude who is the mole with the information we have. We have to investigate very carefully and save King Tritan. This evening, we shall analyze the ring we found in the infinite palace.'

Soon we left the room and walked all over the palace. We spoke with many guards and gathered more information. We had lunch with King Marino and in the evening, we returned to our rooms. I took the ring from my pocket and placed it on a table. Cali asked me how to analyze it. 'Princess, do you have a strategy?'

'Nothing Cali, but I have an idea, I don't know if it will work, but we shall give it a try.' I took the most powerful gadget I had, our handy icy screen. I placed the ring on it, especially the edges and corners. I asked the screen to analyze the data in the ring. The screen didn't respond and nothing was analyzed. Cali gave me the idea to remove the gem from the ring and try once more.

I removed the gem and placed on the screen in all possible locations that I have ever known to analyze anything using the screen. I tried in many ways and didn't get any results. So I got fed up with that ring and threw it on the table in front of me.

After some time, Cali was walking to and fro for ideas to decode the gem. She suddenly shouted, 'Hey Princess, did you observe this? Look at the table and what you have done. You almost found the answer to this mystery gem and the ring.

I looked and was surprised that the gem I had thrown onto the table had fallen onto my precious gems. It was attached to one of the gems I had acquired from the caves mountain Kea. I took it into my hands. I placed the two gems on the edge of the screen and now asked the screen for the data.

It soon started to show me the data that leads to the King. He had been taken to the infinite palace to the one hundred and eighth floor, gradually by climbing ten floors each day. From there, they recently moved to a bubble area. At last, the screen showed us the information recorded in this gem. We both were very happy to have cracked the gem and found solid clues about the King.

I said to Cali, 'Do not share this information with anyone, including King Marino, and the Grand Advisor. Make the necessary arrangements for our travel to that bubble. Our itinerary should be very confidential. Milo should know only that we are leaving tomorrow morning from here to our new destination.'

She nodded her head and went outside the room for the necessary arrangements for our travel. I called the guards and informed them that I wanted to meet King Marino right now.

They soon went to him, and in no time he was here. Now that only we two were there in the room and I said, 'Marino, listen carefully. Tomorrow morning we are leaving from here in search of your father. Be careful and take care of your mother. We will be back as soon as possible.'

He asked, 'Where are you going? Let me come with you.' I said, 'No, my dear, I cannot say everything to you at this moment, but you should take care of this palace and the kingdom. Last time, I gave you my word that you would come with us one time and we took you to the infinite palace. For now, do not ask me anything more. The less you know, the safer you are. '

He reluctantly nodded his head and said, 'Take whatever you want from here and as many men you need. Utilize any resources at hand for this mission. I hope to meet my father soon.' I smiled at him, blinked, and placed my left hand on his shoulder. After a couple of minutes, he wished me the best of luck and walked away. For the remaining part of the day, I didn't move from my room. I thought deeply about our upcoming journey.

Cali came back and I told to her everything. She said, 'Princess, I have informed Milo and the assistants to be ready early in the morning and also never to disclose anything about this mission even to Alton and Brooklyn. The travel arrangements are done and I have enquired about the route and the time it takes. We have to travel almost one and half day to two days depending upon our speed.'

'Okay, fine, Cali, get some rest and we will start early in the morning. We both slept that night and woke early. We were ready for our new mission. No one knew about it and we had no visitors for the day. We reached the place for our departure and found the carriage ready for the journey.

Milo and the four assistants were waiting for us. They welcomed me to get into the carriage. This time, Cali had renovated the carriage and it looked way more beautiful than the one we had previously traveled in.

As usual, Cali took the reins and our journey started toward the bubble. We traveled for almost three to four hours. Slowly Milo turned towards me and said, 'Shall we take a break Princess, I am starving. We have some special dishes here with some precious and rarely found seafood."

I said, 'Oh, I am sorry. I forgot about that. Cali, stop the carriage and make the arrangements for food preparation.' She nodded and stopped at a beautiful place where the small colored fish were playing in groups around a small mountain with many small trees, colorful bushes, and caves on it.

I took a small walk around the mountain along with Cali and said to her, 'Shall we go inside these caves and find what is there.' She replied, 'As you wish, my dear Princess. We both are always ready for an adventure.'

We both slowly walked into the cave. It had a medium size opening and was glowing brightly. It looked very small from the outside, but it is very big on the inside. There were many openings coming off the main corridor. We took the first left and started walking. We came to know all the passages finally lead to one way. That path led us to a particular place where some men were guarding a treasure box.

We slowly moved towards them. They saw us and pointed their spears while asking loudly, 'Who are you? What do you want? This place is forbidden for visitors. You should leave immediately.'

Cali replied to them, 'We are citizens of Aqualean and she is the Princess of Aqualean.' Suddenly, the guards bowed in apology.

I said, 'Guards, who are you? Do you know me?' They replied, 'We are the guards of this treasure box that belongs to Aqualean. We are citizens of Aqualean wearing the uniforms of Aqualean soldiers.

Cali soon saw their uniforms. Some parts looked like Aqualean with the spikes circle used now. I asked, 'What is that box? Why are you wearing this uniform?'

One of the guards replied, 'We are the protectors of this box. We stay in the village nearby this mountain. In fact, all the villagers are responsible for its protection. Our ancestors started protecting this box and thereafter, we took charge. Every month we receive gems and food from Aqualean for our duty here. '

I was surprised and asked Cali about it. Her face turned into a question mark. I understood that she didn't know anything about this, I ordered Cali to call Milo to get clarity on this issue. Now Milo and Cali were in the cave. I turned towards Milo and signaled him with my eyes, 'What is the matter?'

He replied, 'Princess, I too don't know much about this, but every month we send food and gems. It is said that this started long back...maybe centuries ago. I believe nobody knows it. It became a tradition passed on from generation to generation.'

I asked the guards to open the box for me. They refused and said, 'Princess, this box is not only protected by us but also by an invisible force. Only the royal family members of Aqualean - especially the King, Prince, or Princess - can only touch it.

If anyone else tries to touch it, they will faint and remain unconscious for at least a week. The box's weight will be different for royal family members compared to any others.

It will be very heavy for others and very light for Aqualean royal family members.'

As the Princess of the Aqualean, I assumed I could touch the box and open it. The guard replied, 'Yes, definitely, my dear Princess, you can take it with you. I just want you to retain security.'

I slowly moved towards the box and touched it with my right hand. It started to glow. I took the box into my hands and opened it. I was surprised to see gold foil rolled and tied with a silver ribbon and a letter for the person who had opened it.

I placed the box back in its location, took the letter, and opened it. I started studying the letter. Strangely, it had been written to me long back even though it didn't mention any name. I felt deeply connected to it. I read the letter out loud so that others could hear it. *Dear protector of Aqualean, if you are reading this letter then you are in search of something or someone. This gold foil will help you in your time of utmost need. Once the foil is removed from the box, a new foil will appear in a month. Use the foil wisely and bring peace upon the Ocean world.*

I folded the letter and placed it in the box. I took the rolled golden foil and untied the silver ribbon. Slowly I unrolled the foil, but there was nothing on it. The foil was blank. I showed it to Cali. They were equally surprised. I carefully rolled the gold foil and placed it in my bag. I kept the box in its position and said to the guards to come and meet me in the Aqualean palace after two weeks.

We went back to our camping area and enjoyed delicious food before packing everything for our further journey to the bubble. We had traveled more than halfway when Cali said we should halt for the whales to get some rest.

I said to her, 'Okay, Cali, stop the carriage in a safe place. We shall halt here for this night.' She stopped the carriage in a plain. I created a strong and beautiful bubble with ample amount of space to walk in. We spent the night and started our journey the next day. We traveled for half a day to reach our destination. Finally, Cali stopped the carriage a little distance from the bubble. We could see it from our location.

I got down first and stood beside the carriage. I looked keenly at this unique bubble. It was a 'bubbles bubble.' Small bubbles were moving randomly. From certain angles, they depicted the colors of a larger bubble. These all bubbles were encapsulated into a large bubble, like our kingdom.

I said to Cali, 'Get ready with all the gadgets and tools. We shall not waste time standing here, my dear.' In no time Cali, Milo, and the remaining members were ready. We walked slowly while observing the pattern of the bubbles for any other clues for decoding them. Our efforts were in vain. No one on the team could figure out any regularity in their movements. So, we decided to move inside the main bubble to find a clue to crack the puzzle.

Cali entered first. I followed along with Milo and the remaining members in a row. From the inside, it was very beautiful - beyond our expectations. There were no buildings inside the bubble. Rather, it was like a sort of garden, one I hadn't ever seen.

The smaller bubbles were transparent, each outlined with a different color while some were multi-color. As of now, we all were safe and together. I ordered Milo to divide the team into two groups and search in the garden for King Tritan. One bubble came towards us. Everyone moved away because we still didn't know what would happen if it touched us. We just missed the touch since it moved more towards Milo. In fact, I thought it touched Milo.

Our happiness didn't last for long. Very soon, two randomly moving bubbles moved towards us. One of them touched one of our assistants. He disappeared causing our great surprise. We searched but we couldn't find him. Now we had to search for two people.

Cali, one assistant and I formed one group while Milo and the other two assistants formed another one. We decided to go in different directions. As yet, we hadn't moved much and could see each other. Suddenly a bubble moved toward Milo and he came into contact with it. He also disappeared. I called upon the remaining members and said, 'Be careful, stick together and watch each other's backs from these dangerous bubbles moving randomly.'

Within no time, the bubble touched Cali and an assistant. Soon a bubble moved toward me and touched me. From here my analysis started. At first, I felt bad, but I knew where I was. I was in the bubble and found some interesting things about bubbles. When a bubble touches a person, it will encapsulate him and no one will know it since the bubble will still be transparent. The person in the bubble can see the other bubbles and also the persons outside them. They cannot hear us and we were not able to control the direction of the bubble.

I shouted a lot, but the people standing outside couldn't hear me. A little later, all the assistants were encapsulated. We could not see the other people in their bubbles. Even after encapsulation, the bubble appears transparent from the outside. I could see the persons standing outside the bubble but not the persons in the bubbles. No matter their transparency, they all looked alike.

I tried all possible ways with my gems to get out of my bubble. The bubble didn't burst to let me out of it. The bubble was moving here and there around the garden. I slept in it for a couple of hours and thought deeply about an escape plan. I got an idea. I woke up and took out the gems given to me by my father, Queen Aspen and also the gems I have brought from the caves in the mountain.

I held three powerful gems and closed my eyes. I asked the Ocean god to merge the nearest bubble with mine. Soon both bubbles became a larger bubble. Now I had the confidence that I could bring everyone out of these mysterious bubbles. I prayed for the merger of all the bubbles into the outside bubble. I slowly opened my eyes and looked around. The most beautiful thing happened in front of me. All the bubbles had merged into the outer bubble, and we all fell onto the Ocean bed.

Now I could see everyone on our team. We composed ourselves and I asked everyone if they were okay. Everyone said they were fine. Cali asked me what had happened and why the bubbles disappeared?'

'It's a long story that I will explain to you in detail in the carriage,' I said. 'Now let's search for King Tritan. We are now one team. In no time, Milo observed a carriage far away and started moving away from the giant bubble. We soon got into our carriage and followed it although it was very far and moving fast. After traveling for a couple of hours, we lost them. I believed that king Tritan was in that carriage.

SIX

NO WHERE TO SEE

We traveled non-stop in the direction they went. It was almost midnight. Cali suggested to stop the carriage and start our journey in the morning as the persons we were chasing were not visible. We would track them tomorrow. I agreed and everyone went into deep sleep except Cali and me. She came to me and said, 'Do we have anything to do? Why aren't you sleeping?

I told her a secret that no one knew except me and one other person. She was surprised and said, 'Come on, Princess, have so many secrets.' I smiled at her and said, 'Not much, my dear Cali. This one is a little different, and you will be surprised after knowing the secret.'

I took the icy screen in my hands and asked it to track the person who had arranged the tracker. The screen started searching and very soon it tracked that person. I was not surprised to know that the person was in the location toward which we were heading. Cali was also surprised to see the tracker and she bombarded me with questions like 'Who is the person?' Why do you suspect him? When did you fix the tracker? Who fixed the tracker? Please explain to me, Princess.'

I said, 'Relax, Cali, I will explain everything. I arranged the tracker a day before our travel to the bubbles bubble. I didn't do it myself. I had the help of King Marino. Do you want to know who the mole of Tritas kingdom is?' She eagerly said yes. 'He is none other than the Grand Advisor'

She was shocked and said that we should not believe anyone completely in life. 'We should be friendly with everyone but not share everything. This is a classic example. On our first two missions he took part in the planning and he knows everything about our journey. That is why our first two missions failed.'

I said, 'Yes, Cali. We involved him and he managed to escape. This time no one from Tritas knows except the four assistants and King Marino. Moreover, I handed over the tracker gem to Marino to fix on the Grand advisor and he did. Now you can see the result.'

'I suspected him because, on our first two missions, we failed. Especially on the second mission to the infinite palace when we missed him, which means somebody had informed him about their escape. So I decided to keep our every move secretive, and here is the result.'

We took some rest that night. It was almost morning, and we started our journey toward the tracker point shown on the screen. Finally, we drew very near the spot. I said to Cali to stop the carriage far away because we could see some kind of bubble. Cali stopped the carriage and informed everyone to look at the bubble. I saw the bubble keenly but didn't get much data.

We got down from the carriage and slowly walked towards the bubble. We observed that the alligator had just moved out from the bubble and was on his sled. Cali turned towards me and said, 'Look, Princess, the alligator is escaping. I think now we know we are at the correct location.'

I said to Cali, 'Yes, my dear, what you said is right. We are at the correct location, but I don't think the alligator is escaping from us. They don't know yet we are here, so maybe just finished his work or giving his instructions. I think he will be moving to his den. Now, let's move closer to the bubble and observe it from the outside. The bubble looks like a medium size kingdom. I think it is newly restructured by the alligator from stolen gems from the rich and prosperous kingdoms.'

We are very close to the bubble and could see everything. It looked very beautiful inside. There was a palace we had never seen and a village beside it. We couldn't spot anyone outside the palace or village.

I said to my team members, 'Is everyone ready for the final combat in the rescue of King Tritan.' All the team members shouted a very big, yes. We moved to the bottom of the bubble and entered it. Every one of us was surprised after entering the bubble as we could not spot buildings and structures now. Literally, there is nothing inside the bubble. Milo moved forward and discovered the mystery.

He was hit by something and fell. He came back and said, 'Princess, I was hit by some wall structure invisible to us.' We moved back to the outside. Now we could clearly see everything inside the bubble. 'We have to go with a plan otherwise, we will end up in their trap. I have an idea for this problem.'

The solution was that one of our assistants would remain to guide us through a dedicated communication channel. Milo said, 'Good one, Princess. That was a very fast and optimal solution.' He ordered one of the assistants to stay there. Now we started moving inside the bubble. As expected, we saw nothing. Cali connected to the assistant, who guided us to move inside the bubble to the palace which is at the center of the bubble.

The assistant said that we were at the entrance of the palace and instructed us to move ahead directly so we could go. As per his guidance, we moved forward confidently. My plan worked and we were in. We could see everything from inside the palace. It was very beautiful from the inside. We started searching for King Tritan. Very soon we entered a huge hall. Finally, we found King Tritan sitting on a chair. Likely, he couldn't move away from it.

The mole of the kingdom Tritan, the Grand advisor, was beside him. Plus, there were more than ten others around them, maybe the guards of the palace. Before I said a word, the Grand advisor spoke, 'Welcome, Princess. You have finally found us. It was inevitable - and so fast.'

'You have underestimated us and now we are here to take the king back and put you where you belong. He replied, 'That's impossible, my dear Princess. This place is not Aqualean or Tritas. I have modified it recently, especially for our future requirements. We assure you that we are strong and stubborn.'

I laughed at him and said, 'You are actually in a very weak building because we got in very fast in no time. Good will win over evil every time, but it may take some time, depending upon the circumstances.'

He said those statements are trash, now I will make you all my prisoners in no time. I said, 'Don't dream big. The result will be out very soon, so don't waste our time. Hand over King Tritan peacefully and surrender yourself.'

He laughed and said that he would fight and win this battle easily. He would impress the alligator and get more rewards. The Grand Advisor threw a gem in the middle of the hall. It had been a couple of minutes and nothing happened. He was smiling at us. Though nothing happened, I suspected that something strange already happened that we hadn't recognized. He ordered the guards to capture us.

The guards started moving towards us. I took a red gem into my hand and tried to freeze them. It didn't work moreover I observed that there was no glow in the gem. The Advisor laughed loudly at me and said he had frozen all the gem powers and I am out of moves. A guard came to us and I looked at Milo and signaled him to defend us until we could find a solution. Milo and the assistants fought fiercely. Meanwhile, Cali and I moved aside and hid behind a pillar.

I took the gems one by one and tried to use them, but my actions were of no use; none of them glowed. While I was trying to figure out a solution, I heard the Grand Advisor's voice saying, 'Princess, your gem power will not work here. Take your time and try all the gems you have with you. Then you can finally surrender.

I was thinking deeply about how to bring back the powers of the gems. I took the icy screen out and held it in front of me. I hadn't asked anything but it was showing a gem at the center of the screen. I understood. I said to Cali, 'Look, Cali, we can see the image of the gem defending our powers, which means this screen can do something for us.

Cali asked the screen a tricky question, 'Oh my screen, do we have anything with us now to get our gem powers back?' Now I was surprised to see that the screen showed a scroll. Cali said, 'Princess, I believe that this scroll may be the golden scroll we grabbed recently from a cave.' Soon I took the scroll into my hands and opened it.

The icy screen was on my lap and the scroll was in my hand. I placed the scroll on the screen for support. This unexpected move revealed a secret that would nullify the defending power of the gem used by the Grand Advisor.

Why I am still calling him Grand Advisor, now I would call him the mole. I showed the images on the golden scroll to Cali after placing it on the icy screen without any intervention. Cali had gone through it and said, 'What do you understand by this? Nothing is here except the gem and a line.

I said to Cali, 'Look, my dear, when we took it from the box, we were informed that this scroll could help us when in need. Now we are in need and haven't asked for help this time. It means this scroll will give us the optimum solution at the optimal time.

Cali said, 'I didn't infer anything from this image. Maybe I need to become accustomed to image solutions.'

'Yes, my dear, that is my inference from this image. The gem shown here is the gem thrown by the mole, and the line above the gem I believe is the earth, which means burying the gem in the earth is the solution.'

Soon Cali ran towards the center of the hall where everyone was busy fighting. Cali approached the gem, took it into her hands and started running outside the palace. She ran very fast and placed the gem on the ground and covered it with soil. Instantly, all my gems started glowing. I was happy that all my powers were back. The first thing I did was to destroy the defending gem, using my red power gem. Slowly, I moved toward the center of the hall and said, 'You culprits, my powers are back and your gem is destroyed.'

The Grand Advisor asked me how that had happened. 'I didn't even know how to do it. I agree that you are a genius, my dear Princess, but I still can defend you by myself. I have so many new power gems from the great alligator.'

I know very well that culprits have alternative plans, but ultimately, victory will be always with me. He took another gem into his hands and pointed to the roof. Soon a hole formed for the bubble. A water jet came from it, but the water didn't flow. The water jet, however, pointed towards us and waited for his instructions.

He directed the water jet toward my team, and everyone fell apart. We couldn't manage to even stand properly as it began hitting us with a huge force. Again, I went behind the pillar to find an idea to stop this water jet. I placed the scroll on the screen and got a simple answer. There were images of water and ice. I understood that I had to convert the water into ice. Water will listen to him, but ice will not, given the kind of gem power he had.

Soon, I took the gem given to me by Queen Aspen into my hands and prayed that the water controlled by him would convert into ice immediately. I peeked out from beside the pillar and was glad to see that the water had indeed converted into ice. It was amazing! The mole tried and tried to control the ice but he failed. We all assembled and Milo asked, 'Princess, we are always in defense mode, When shall we capture him.' I said, 'Very soon, Milo.

During this short exchange, the mole started a new game. He threw a gem on the floor; soon it became a pedestal of around four feet in height. Three hands emerged from it. It started rotating very fast and throwing gems at us. We all hid behind the pillars. Cali and I signaled everyone not to take any action and try to stay protected. It continued to rain gems. Later, I observed that it was not randomly throwing gems at us but was constructing a gem wall around them.

In no time, the King and all the kidnappers were enclosed in a huge chamber of gems. This was unexpected because until now, we had been encapsulated. Now they had encapsulated themselves. After some time, the gem-throwing activity stopped. We came out and walked around the new gem room. The room was huge —almost equal to the size of the hall. Milo and the assistants tried to break the room walls with physical force, but nothing happened. I used my gems to open the gem wall for us but we ended up in vain. The walls were strong and stubborn.

As usual, I opened the golden scroll for a solution. The solution was to add more gems without breaking the closed-loop structure. It means that the gems couldn't be destroyed and the seal can't be broken by any external force. So use extra gems to get inside externally. I called upon everyone and made a gem room for us. I attached it to the already encapsulated room structure. Now the entire structure was sealed. I tried to open the gems of the large room from the small room.

Surprisingly, the gems moved very easily with my gem power and we easily entered the encapsulated large room. I could see that the culprits were packing up for their escape. The mole was shocked and told me, 'You are solving every puzzle, Princess. This is the last one and we are out of this palace.'

He took another gem and threw it on the floor quickly. Soon the room was filled with some kind of sponge-like material. We could not see each other or hear our voices. I believed he was escaping with King Tritan. I made some space by pushing some of the sponge material to the side, and I sat on the floor. To clear it manually could take hours, but I knew there would be a remedy. I opened the golden scroll again.

This time the solution was very dangerous. The scroll showed the sponge versus fire. I understood that this sponge was flammable. I had the solution! I took the blue sapphire gem into my hands and prayed for ice encapsulation for everyone in the sponge, including the culprits and the King. After encapsulation, I set all the sponge material on fire.

I was encapsulated and believed everyone was. Soon the fire burned the entire sponge. Now I could see that our team members were safe and sound. Oddly enough, only my team members were encapsulated.

Cali asked, 'Princess, why to encapsulate only our members?' I said, 'No, my dear, I asked for everyone's encapsulation as they might have escaped.' All the team members came out of the ice encapsulation and searched the entire palace thoroughly but found no one. They could have escaped with King Tritan. Cali and Milo were worried that we had missed him.

I walked towards the throne and sat on it. I said, 'Don't worry, my dear team members, this time victory shall be ours soon. Cali asked. 'How, my dear Princess? Did you attach a new tracker on the King? Or did you send someone behind them?'

I just smiled and said, 'Our work is done here. We shall leave this palace and also this bubble. They will come to us very soon.' I walked out of the palace with all the team members following me. In no time, we reached the point where we had entered and met our assistant there.

Now Cali's and Milo's anticipation could be tamed. The hero of this battle was the giant whale. Milo said, 'Princess, are we going on it to chase them?' I laughed and said, 'Not required, Milo. They are here. Cali asked me, 'Where, Princess? I cannot see them, so please don't prolong the suspense.'

I clapped at the giant whale and it opened its mouth. All the culprits and the King spat out and fell on the ground in front of us. All the members clapped at my move. Soon

Milo and the assistants ran toward the King and took care of him. I bowed before him, and said, 'Uncle Tritan, King of Tritas.'

He came toward me and caught my shoulders with both hands. He made me stand and said, 'Princess Adira, you are grown, and you saved my life. I have to bow before you, I owe you my life.'

I said no, 'Uncle, definitely not. We are one family and will be like that forever.' I said to Milo, 'Arrange for our travel to Tritas kingdom, we shall go in the carriage. You and a couple of assistants come with the culprits in the giant whale's mouth.' He nodded and arranged everything. We traveled for almost one day to reach the kingdom of Tritas Finally, we were at the entrance. I got down first and the remaining members including the King followed.

The security at the entrance saw us as well as the King. A loud trumpet sound was the sign of entry for us. Usually, this sound was made during happy moments in the kingdom or the arrival of an allied king. Now, these sounds were for us. In no time, Marino and his mother came, followed by relatives and other officials, including Brooklyn and Alton. Marino and his mother hugged the King, crying with happiness.

Slowly everyone moved into the palace. The culprits were taken care of by Brooklyn and his team. Everyone could now relax. I met the king along with Milo and Cali personally in his meeting room. I asked King Tritan what had happened and why he had been kidnapped. Was the Grand Advisor involved? He turned towards me and thanked me a lot for my courageous rescue operation

He said, 'My dear Adira, it's a very long and complicated story, I will simplify it. Tritas is a very rich nation because of its gem forest and also the knowledge we possess in terms of treasures. Every King of Tritas has more responsibilities than a normal king. We have to safeguard that information.

'I was kidnapped by the evil alligator with the help of our Grand Advisor. Neither the Grand Advisor nor the alligator was involved directly in the actual kidnapping. When I am walking in the palace corridors with the Grand Advisor and Brooklyn, suddenly I was encapsulated in an invisible gem chamber and taken from here.'

'As the chamber was invisible, no one could see me. At that time, even I did not know that our Grand Advisor was involved. I was taken to the infinite palace via the gem forest. First, I was on the tenth floor, and then each day I was taken ten to fifteen floors up. They used their powers on me so I couldn't move from my chair. Finally, I was placed on the hundred and eighth floor.'

'There I came to know that our Grand Advisor was involved in my kidnapping. He was bribed by the alligator with a huge amount of gems along with the Tritas kingdom and his youth-ness back. I mean a reversal of his age. Later, I was moved to bubbles-bubble, where you had searched for me. But they had moved me to the palace where you rescued me. They wanted information regarding the conversion of a powerful javelin into a powerful trident. The alligator wanted the exact location to get such a trident. With that trident, he could become the King of the Ocean. No one could defeat him with that trident in his hand. He tried to get more information, but I wouldn't open my mouth for him or the Grand Advisor.

"Finally, you have rescued me and brought me back to my kingdom. Thank you, everyone, for saving me and the entire world."

I stood and said, "Take care, my King. Please give us permission to leave for Aqualean. He said, 'In a couple of days I am arranging a party on my arrival. So please be here for the party.' We nodded our heads and took the leave for the day from him.

A Small Favor Requested

Thank you very much for choosing my book. This is my second book in this alligator series. If you have enjoyed the story, please rate this book so that I can be encouraged; It will help me progress on my author journey. Your feedback means a lot to me. So, kindly take the time to rate it.

Thank you once again!

www.ingramcontent.com/pod-product-compliance
Lightning Source LLC
Chambersburg PA
CBHW031434130726
47989CB00003B/1143